CRUELTY TO INNOCENTS

Cruelty to Innocents

The First Novel in the 911 Abduction Series

By CK Webb & DJ Weaver

CRUELTY TO INNOCENTS

The First Novel in the 911 Abduction Series

by

CK Webb and DJ Weaver

PRINT EDITION

* * * * *

PUBLISHED BY:

WebbWeaver

PUBLISHING HISTORY

Suspense Publishing, digital edition/May 2011

ISBN-13: 978-0615508764

ISBN-10: 0615508766

CRUELTY TO INNOCENTS

CRUELTY TO INNOCENTS

EARLY PRAISE FOR
CRUELTY TO INNOCENTS

"A kidnapped child is every parent's worst nightmare—but imagine how you'd feel if your daughter were snatched away while you were distracted trying to save someone else's life. Set in the sort of town where we all take safety for granted, *The 911 Abductions* is a heart wrenching, emotional roller coaster readers won't soon forget."

–TASHA ALEXANDER, BESTSELLING AUTHOR OF "DANGEROUS TO KNOW"

"A girl goes missing…and time is running out in this explosive debut novel by CK Webb and DJ Weaver. "Cruelty to Innocents" is a riveting thriller that ratchets up the adrenaline and forces you to turn the pages faster and faster as you hope for the best, while fearing the worst. This is a poignant, big-hearted novel that finds good in the midst of evil, hope in the midst of despair. Cruelty will touch your heart and give you plenty to think about after the last page has been turned."

–JOHN LOCKE, BESTSELLING AUTHOR OF "SAVING RACHEL"

"Let me say "Cruelty to Innocents" is not a very long book but it is long enough to knock your socks off!

CRUELTY TO INNOCENTS

I love, love, love the characters in the book. Sloanne is an amazing woman who faces her demons by going back to Aberdeen Maryland, a place she left and had no intentions of returning to. She does, to help her best friend, Chloe find her missing daughter, Sloanne's god-daughter. Once back she pairs up with Shawn Tyler, a local fireman and old school acquaintance. The two of them together are such fun to follow as they do everything they can to find the missing girl. Sloanne and Shawn are two people that I would love to have as neighbors!

Twists and turns aplenty in "Cruelty to Innocents." It will have you up well into the wee hours turning pages and wanting more. I was floored by the ending and never suspected what was coming. CK Webb and DJ Weaver are authors you don't want to miss. If you love suspense hurry up and grab this book. Highly recommended."

–REVIEWED BY KENDALL GUTIERREZ (http://readingreadingandlife.blogspot.com)

To our families, friends, colleagues and supporters...
Love and thanks to each of you.

To those who said it could not be done,
thank you for the inspiration,
we could not have done it without you.

For Matt,
we did it!

CRUELTY TO INNOCENTS

PROLOGUE

I hear it beckoning me from the other room, the faint crackle of my scanner as it comes to life. Something is happening somewhere; a car wreck, a shooting, an emergency. She is there all alone. I know it. The ones who are supposed to love and protect her are busy trying to help complete strangers. They are trying to save the life of others, but they are neglecting the one they should be watching over. They have forgotten her, left her…forsaken her. I race to the scene, my mind tearing me in two directions.

One side says, *'Not again'*. But the other side screams, begs, *'Please, just one more'*. That voice muffles out the cries of the other and wins again. It always wins.

I have to be quick. I pan the crowd searching for her. The blood pounds in my ears and my breath is ragged and quick. All other sounds slip away. I search the crowd with starving eyes. Where is she? I can't find her. Wait…there…she is all alone and so beautiful. She needs me. I see the purity in her eyes, the longing. She is a good girl. I won't have to punish her like the others. She will be different. She is so beautiful. I promise myself she will be the last. I have to have her, just one more. I wait for the perfect moment to take her away from all this. No one is watching as I make my way through the crowd of gaping onlookers. Stealthily, quickly, I am beside her. She looks up with loving, innocent eyes and smiles just for me. '*Now*'! My mind screams. '*Take her*'. I turn to embrace her and she is mine.

ONE

Taken

Chloe Jacobs sighed and clinched the steering wheel tighter as her daughter continued to badger her about the un-chaperoned sleep-over. A sleepover Chloe had no intention of letting her daughter attend that night.

"Why can't I go to the party? All the other girls are going and I want to go too. This is not fair, Mother," Chloe's beautiful, thirteen-year-old daughter Danielle, barked at her mom.

Danni was being relentless on this sleep-over conversation and Chloe endured about all of this subject she could. As Danni talked, she was compulsively flipping through the stations on the radio, which made the tension in the car even more unbearable. The two were making their way to the local Klein's Super Market in Chloe's late-model Honda.

Chloe considered herself to be the typical, single parent. She was thirty-one-years old, but still young enough to remember what it was like to be thirteen. All of those feelings you have as a thirteen-year-old, always feeling like everything is so permanent. She knew Danni believed it would be the end of the world if she didn't attend the party. When Chloe was thirteen, she believed she knew everything about life: how it worked and how it would turn out. She realized now that she was older, how very wrong she had been. How could she make her daughter understand there would be many more big events in her life? Chloe just wanted Danni to slow down and enjoy being a kid.

Many people considered Chloe a classic beauty with her long, flaxen-blond hair and pale, crystal-blue eyes, all of which still drew the occasional wolf-whistle from men on the street. Those that knew her thought of her as an intelligent, responsible and well-put-together person who made a wonderful home for her only daughter.

Her full-time job with the Aberdeen Family Medical Clinic demanded long working hours and with a teen-age daughter to raise, that left little time for dating. Chloe knew there was no room in their life for a relationship and for now she was content.

"Danni, you are not going to an all-nighter without chaperones and that's final," Chloe said for the umpteenth time.

Danni wrinkled up her face and slumped down in her seat while giving her mom that, 'I am old enough to do what I want' look. Since Danni hit her teens, it was not unusual for them to have these stand-offs over boundary issues, but when push came to shove, Danni was a good kid who minded her mother and was always there when Chloe needed her.

The crime rate in Aberdeen was low and it had always been a relatively safe town. Nothing bad ever happened to disturb the quiet peacefulness and it was small enough to allow local law enforcement to keep a watchful eye on everything. The kids who were planning to attend the party would be safe enough, but this wasn't about safety. This was about boundaries and Danni needed to learn hers.

"I hate you when you act like I am a baby, Mom," her daughter huffed with a big pout on her face. "I'm not your little girl anymore. I'm thirteen and I know what's happening—stop treating me like a child. I wish Dad was here."

Danni knew how badly Chloe hated it when her father's name was thrown into these conversations and Chloe was convinced Danni did it for that very reason. This was one of Danni's manipulations and Chloe recognized it all too well. Danni did it just to make Chloe feel bad in the hope that she would give in. But, Danni's dad wasn't there and Chloe refused to feel guilty...not this time.

"Danni, if you mention this party one more time, I swear you will be sitting in your room until you are at least thirty. Now get over it." Chloe said almost gritting her teeth.

Danni ignored her mom as she stared out the car window at the local scenery. Chloe hoped that would end the conversation. She longed for the days when Danni was easier to get along with.

They passed the outlet mall on I-95, the main highway that ran through Aberdeen Maryland and pulled into the grocery store parking lot. As they got out, Danni rolled her eyes and looked over at her mom with a pout on her face. *So much like her dad*, Chloe thought to herself. Great. Just what she needed, both Danni *and* her ex-husband giving her the evil eye all the way through the grocery store. During moments like these—when Danni was being a defiant teenager—motherhood was the most difficult. Chloe sighed to herself as she thought.

"Well, since I'm stuck at home tonight while everyone else is at the party, can we at least have pizza for dinner and maybe pick up a movie?"

Danni flipped her hair back in that charming way she had and just like a puff of smoke, her attitude disappeared. It was as if the conversation never took place at all.

"Good idea. Can we have mushrooms on the pizza?" Chloe now beamed at her daughter

"Eeewww...how about mushrooms on *half* the pizza...your half."

Danni did a little happy dance into the store.

They started their rounds through the store as usual: cereal, milk, butter, eggs and pizza fixings. These trips to the grocery usually made Danni happy because she liked picking out ingredients for her next 'masterpiece'. That's what she called the crazy recipes she would throw together on her own and serve whenever her mother was late from work. Mostly the meals were pretty good with the occasional flop, but all in all, Danni was turning out to be a fairly good cook. Today, Chloe could see her daughter was really into it, no longer worrying about the sleep-over business.

They began to talk about things at school. Danni told her mom about the new girl with a nose ring and tattoo. Danni proceeded to tell Chloe about the tattoo she wanted for herself. Chloe cringed at the thought.

"I think a small angel on the back of my neck would be awesome," Danni beamed at her mom.

Chloe smiled, but tried not to encourage or discourage her daughter. There had been enough bickering for one day and she really wanted Danni to be happy.

"I think an angel would be okay, but maybe you should wait a few years before making any major decisions. I used to like frogs when I was your age, but can you imagine me with a big, frog tattoo now. That would be too funny," Chloe teased and they both laughed at the imagined sight of Kermit tattooed on Chloe.

They made their way up and down the aisles as they continued to laugh and talk. As Chloe turned her cart to start down the next aisle, she noticed an older man a few feet away with a contorted look of pain on his face. She saw this just as he put one hand out to grab the end cap he was standing by, while his other hand went to his chest. He made a grating sound in his throat and his face twisted into an awful grimace that told Chloe he was definitely in trouble. She stepped towards the man to ask if she could help just as his body stiffened and started to fall. Chloe knew she'd never be able to catch the guy, but tried to at least, break his fall. He must have out-weighed her by one hundred pounds and despite her attempts to help, the man hit the floor hard, taking out the end cap display as he fell. Bags of chips, pretzels and tortillas crashed to the floor along with the shelving as the man toppled over.

Vaguely remembering her CPR training, Chloe pulled the man's head back and listened for breath sounds, but heard none. Her heart began to race and her adrenaline shot up. She checked for a pulse, but found nothing there either. She heard Danni ask if the man was dead, but Chloe could only focus on helping the stranger. She did not reply to her daughter. Chloe screamed for anyone in the gathering crowd of shoppers to call 9-1-1 and began giving the man breaths of air as best she could. It felt as if time stopped as she frantically tried to resuscitate the old man. She knew she should be pumping his chest as well, but panic was enveloping her and her mind no longer felt connected to her body.

She frantically scanned the crowd, searching for anyone who could help. A young man she knew as one of the store's stock boys stepped out of the crowd and bent down to the old man. He immediately began giving the man chest compressions as Chloe counted out the breaths she was administering. Hours passed by in minutes. Somewhere in Chloe's head, she heard the sound of whining—or was it sirens?

"Here come the paramedics," Chloe heard someone say. She

was running out of air as two men materialized beside her and began to work on the old man without missing a beat. Chloe stood up and stepped aside so both paramedics could get to the victim. The scene before her took on a surreal feeling, as if she were watching a movie. She vaguely heard Charlie, the store manager, say something about her quick thinking and good work, but she could not take her eyes from the horrible scene before them. Then, in a commanding voice, Charlie directed the crowd to step back and give the EMTs room to work.

"I've got no breath sounds and no pulse," the EMTs voice was clear and strong over the murmur of the crowd that gathered.

"Charge the paddles to two hundred," the other EMT was already into the bag and charging the portable defibrillator.

"*Clear*," yelled the paramedic and the old man's body jumped.

"Nothing. Charge to three hundred and hit him again."

"*Clear*," yelled the EMT again and the old man's body danced around on the floor like a rag doll.

Chloe began to think the old man was not going to make it. The crowd quieted and she could now hear the soft crying of an older lady behind her. She was still concentrating on the scene before her and could not bring herself to comfort the woman.

"Still nothing. Hit him again."

The EMT charged the paddles to three hundred fifty and

yelled, "*Clear.*"

This time the man's body seemed to come completely off the floor, falling back down with a thump. The EMT again checked the old man's pulse and shook his head.

"This guy is gone, but we need to get him to the Medical Center." The EMT looked at the people standing around and asked, "Does anyone know who this man is?"

A man in the crowd said he thought the gentleman's first name was Homer, but did not know his last name. Chloe noticed there were two police officers standing back from the crowd. Funny, she had not noticed them before, but she assumed they heard the emergency response call and followed in behind the EMTs. She had been so focused on Homer, but now her mind was clearing and Chloe realized Danni was not visible.

"Danni." Chloe called out, but no voice came back to her.

"Danielle, where are you?" Chloe yelled, louder this time and with more force.

As the paramedics loaded the man's body on a gurney and the crowd started to thin, Chloe's eyes scanned the front of the store. She felt a sickening fear rising through her. Where was her daughter?

"Danni! Danielle!"

Chloe looked at every face in the fading crowd and the area all around her. She moved towards her cart and headed to the back of the store. She quickly made her way through the swinging doors that led back in the direction of the stock room. The ladies restroom was the last door on the left. Chloe burst through the door and quickly checked all the stalls, yelling Danni's name as she went. Complete panic was setting in now. Chloe knew her daughter would never intentionally scare her by disappearing this way. Finding no signs of Danni, she turned and flew back towards the front of the store.

The young, stock boy who helped her with the old man was standing close to the front entrance. Chloe jerked him by the arm, spinning him around to quickly ask if he had seen Danni.

"Have you seen my daughter? Have you seen Danni?" she demanded.

The boy's puzzled look made Chloe even more anxious and before he could say anything, Chloe spoke again.

"You've seen her before. You know, thirteen-years-old, about four-eleven, thin build, long, blond hair. She was wearing dark, blue shorts, tennis shoes and a light, blue ball shirt with 'Aberdeen Blue Angels' on the front and #33 on the back."

Halfway through her description, one of the police officers seeing her distress approached her and the young man.

"My name is Officer Parker. Can I help, ma'am?"

"Yes, please. I can't seem to find my daughter. She was standing right here when the gentleman fell and I know she was here part of the time. I was trying to help, but then I lost track of her. It's not like her to just walk away. I don't understand where she could be."

Chloe massaged her temple.

The stock boy began to speak with concern in his voice, "I am sure she was standing right behind you when I first came up to help, but after that I just don't know. I'm sorry. Let me help you look for her."

The officer looked up from his note pad, "Can you give me that description again?"

Chloe ran through it quickly for him. She began to feel a little better. The police would surely find Danni and things would go back to normal. Then, they would go on with their evening as planned.

"I will notify the manager and have him lock down the store. No one in and no one out. My partner and I will check around the back of the store and cruise the parking lot to see if we can find her. She probably just stepped outside. Maybe this whole thing upset her, you know how kids are? You stay close by in case she returns. We'll be back shortly."

The officer then turned to the stock boy and asked him to look around the store for Danni and to notify the other employees to do the same.

"Yes, sir."

The boy quickly spun around and started walking towards the meat department, looking down each aisle as he passed by. He yelled out to the man behind the meat counter, giving him a quick description of Danni. The butcher then turned and started toward the back of the store, relaying the description of the missing girl to the store manager as he passed him. The store manager headed towards the customer service area. Only a few moments passed before Chloe heard him paging Danni over the PA system, requesting she come to the front of the store.

She turned to walk out the front entrance to check whether or not Danni might have gone to the car. When she reached the front door, she was detained by a clerk who informed her she could not leave. The store manager overheard the conversation and informed the clerk Chloe was the missing child's mother and would be the only one permitted to exit or enter the store, besides the police.

By this time, Chloe was starting to freak out. Danni knew how easily she worried and Chloe wondered why her daughter would just disappear without saying a word. Surely Danni hadn't decided to walk home or to a friend's house. *No, she wouldn't do that to me. Would she?* Chloe thought to herself as she scanned the spaces between the parked cars. Her mind raced through every scenario she could think of. *Where could Danni be?*

As she arrived at her car, she could see Danni was nowhere in sight. Panic began to rise again and Chloe felt breathless, almost choking. She pulled out her cell and started thumbing through phone numbers, but thought better of calling anyone. Chloe knew Danni was not the sort of kid who did things like this and now she was even more worried.

Just as she slipped her cell back in her pocket, the two police officers pulled up and Officer Parker—whom Chloe had given the description to—jumped out of the car and came towards her. For the second time today, the minutes moved like hours. Chloe could see a look of dread on the officer's face and she started to shake. Her mind began to race again as the officer strode towards her.

"Ma'am was your daughter wearing any jewelry when you last saw her?" the officer asked with a strange tone in his voice.

"I'm sure she probably had on earrings. Her ears are pierced so she wears them all the time. Why?"

Chloe's voice was shaking now. Blood was pounding in her head. What was happening?

"Anything else? Any other jewelry?" the officer asked again.

The answer flashed through Chloe's mind.

"A watch…a 'Twilight' watch. It has a picture of Edward and Bella on the face. I just bought it for her last week. It's her favorite book and…"

Chloe was breathing too hard and her hands were trembling now, almost uncontrollably. Fear gripped her stomach nearly making her gag.

The look on the officer's face as he held out his hand to her was one Chloe would never forget.

"Is this the watch?"

Chloe's knees started to go weak as the officer spoke.

"Oh my god. Where did you find this? It's Danni's watch! Oh my god! Where is my daughter?" Chloe screamed at the officer.

"We found it around back of the store, ma'am. There were some tire marks in the lot next to where the watch was laying, as if somebody took off in a hurry. We spoke to an older woman who lives next to the back parking lot. She was out in her yard and thinks she saw a dark blue or black car leaving the lot in a hurry. She noticed because she heard the tires squealing," he explained to Chloe.

"We think Danni must have dropped the watch by accident. Is Danni close with her dad? He could have picked her up and she may have dropped the watch while getting in his car. Is that possible?"

"No, no. Danni's dad is gone. There is no one she could have left here with. Her grand parents are dead and besides, Danni would never just leave and not tell me," Chloe stammered.

"Does Danni have a boyfriend? Is there anyone you can think of who she could have gone to visit? Did you two have a fight or disagreement? Maybe she ran off mad or…"

"No! Oh god. Someone must have taken her! Please help me. Someone had to have taken her. She's a good girl. She would never worry me like this. Please help me find her," Chloe begged, beside herself, tears rolling down her face.

Panic tasted like vomit in her mouth and she half fell, half sat down right there in the parking lot. The officer stooped down and touched Chloe's shoulder. He turned his head and silently directed the other officer to call for medical assistance. Chloe's head began to spin and bright flashes of light appeared before her eyes.

"Don't worry now, ma'am. Your daughter is probably just walking around somewhere or heading home. I'll call this in right away. Normally, we don't follow up on these things for a certain period of time, but this watch makes me uneasy. Since you declared there is no one else she could have left with, I'm going to contact my chief who will in turn contact the Detective Division. They will be the ones who will determine whether an *Amber Alert* should be issued. We are going to cordon off the area and radio this in. A detective will be here shortly and we'll start processing the witnesses inside the store. Stranger abductions are considered the most crucial and in those cases time is very important. You should call everyone your daughter might have been in contact with while we wait. Do you feel like you can get up? My partner will help you inside where you'll be more comfortable. After I talk to the chief, I'll be back inside. Do you have a picture of Danni with you, by any chance?"

Chloe then realized she left her purse in the cart she had been pushing in the store.

"I do, but I left my purse inside. Do you really think someone has taken my daughter? But why? Why would anyone want to take Danni? Why?" Chloe cried.

"I don't know, ma'am, but I don't want to take any chances on this. If she shows up, well, that's a good thing, but we have to go at this as what it looks like...an abduction. Now you head inside with Officer George and he'll help you with the phone calls. I'll come in when the detectives arrive. I know this is difficult, but please try not to worry," the officer said. "We're going to do everything we can to get your daughter home safe."

The officer tried to help Chloe up, but by this time she was on the verge of hysteria and could barely stand or speak. She ran the question through her mind. Why would someone take her Danni? She just could not comprehend it. Not her sweet baby girl, Danni. Not her only child. This couldn't be happening...not to Danni...not to her.

Chloe braced herself as Officer George helped her to her feet. They walked around to the front entrance and the store employee opened the door for them. The store manager saw them enter and immediately grabbed a chair for Chloe to sit in. Her mind was so tired. She could barely think as the officer asked her for numbers from her cell phone.

Officer Parker strode to the police cruiser and grabbed the microphone, dread washing over him as he went.

"Central, this is car thirty-six, come back."

"Thirty-six, this is Central, go ahead."

"Central, we have a Code Adam at Klein's Super Market. I need to speak to the chief, ASAP."

"Connecting you now thirty-six, go ahead."

"Chief, this is Parker. We have a Code Adam at Klein's and we need a detective on-scene right away."

"Copy that, Parker. I'll issue a BOLO immediately and send Detective Howard right out. Give me a rundown and description of the victim."

Parker knew a BOLO was a "Be on look out" and exact descriptions were imperative for locating a suspect or victim, but they had very little to go on. Parker ran through the description of Danni and what they found in the parking lot. He also told the chief about the small car that was spotted leaving the scene. The chief assured him Detective Howard would be there in no time and quickly ran through procedures on questioning the witnesses.

Parker had barely hung up the microphone when he heard sirens in the distance getting louder as they approached. What had gone from a 9-1-1 medical emergency call, escalated into something far worse. Parker never worked a kidnapping in Aberdeen and had a bad feeling this was not going to end well.

TWO

Train Ride

Sloanne Mae Kelly's cab stopped short of the unloading area that lined the front curb at sprawling Penn Station. She dropped a twenty dollar bill into the cash slot, said a quick, 'keep the change' and jumped out of the cab, grabbing her two, small bags and her lap top as she went. The train to Aberdeen Maryland would be leaving soon and she had to pick up her ticket before the gates closed. People seemed to sense the urgency in Sloanne's determined look and hurried pace, stepping to the side, allowing her to pass.

Penn Station was a massive, cavernous space that boasted unique architecture and was filled with people of every size, shape and color. The intensity of the noises and smells assaulted Sloanne's senses, making her want to run away, but instead she pressed forward. In her mind, she ran through a million different destinations she would rather be traveling to. Instead, she was heading back home, if home is what it could be called. Her brow tightened at the selfish thoughts. She knew this trip and the circumstances behind it, were all that mattered.

Sloanne held a lucrative position as an interior designer at a top firm in New York City, where she now resided. She loved the city and took advantage of all the things it had to offer. She took Yoga, she went to power lunches and ran in the best circles with some of the city's elite—most days. But this particular day, she was just a girl heading back to her past. Back to a place she would rather not be going. No, she never wanted to return to Aberdeen, but she had to support her best friend who desperately needed her now.

She ran through the station and out onto the platform where her train waited, the day's events thrumming through her head like a hurricane ripping across the shoreline. A knot rose in her throat as she willed back the burning sting of the first tears in her eyes. This day was an unthinkable nightmare, but one she would not awaken from. She stepped onto the train and glanced at her ticket for the seat number: 26A. She turned side-ways, lifting her bag over the other passengers' heads as she made her way to her seat. There was no one in the seat next to hers and for this, she was grateful. The air felt like walls closing in around her on all sides and her mind was overtaken by grief. She placed her bags in the overhead compartment, then took her seat just as her cell phone rang, jolting her out of her thoughts.

Sloanne's assistant Ann, was calling. She left the woman a hasty message to give her a call as soon as possible and now she had to tell her assistant why she would be away for a few days. She would have to acknowledge aloud why she so quickly departed from her job and her life to assist her friend. Sloanne's beautiful, charming, loving goddaughter had been abducted.

"Thank you for getting back to me so quickly," Sloanne

breathed heavy into the receiver.

Her mind rebelled against the story she was about to relate to her assistant and the words were like acid in her throat.

"Ann, I received some terrible news earlier today. I am on my way back to Aberdeen now. My best friend's daughter was abducted and Chloe needs me desperately."

The gasp at the other end of the line told her that her assistant was shocked by what she was hearing. Sloanne kept a lovely picture of Danni on her desk and everyone in the office, including Ann, often commented on what a beautiful girl she was.

"I will need you to cancel all my appointments and forward all my emails to my personal account. Also, please call Mr. Miera and let him know the situation. Tell him I will be in contact with him as soon as I know more. I can't say at this point, how long I'll have to be away, but please reassure him I am holding up as well as can be expected."

The last words faded off to a whisper, as tears slipped from her eyes.

Sloanne thanked Ann for her help and quickly got off the phone. Her head ached as she thought back to the earlier phone call she received. The last time she'd been home was in 2003, to bury her parents. Back then she made a vow: it would be the last time she would ever go back, until today it had been. She kept her word to herself for all these years, but someone had taken her goddaughter.

29

Now she was forced to go back.

At exactly 6:30 p.m. this evening, she received the phone call that no one ever wants to get or imagines possible. Chloe Jacob's neighbor called to say that Chloe's daughter Danielle—or Danni as they liked to call her—had been abducted. Sloanne could barely hold down the hastily-eaten, take-out dinner she ordered earlier in the day. The word tore at her insides: abducted...taken from a grocery store in broad daylight in her own home town. It was not something that ever happened in Aberdeen. Sure, the town had its share of petty crimes, but child abductions were unheard of. In fact, she couldn't remember a single child who had ever been taken from that area.

The one thing that made the events even more unbelievable was the manner in which Danni was abducted. An elderly man suffered a massive heart attack. While Sloanne's best friend worked desperately to help a complete stranger, some asshole helped himself to her daughter.

According to the local authorities and from what she already knew, the first forty-eight hours were the most crucial time period in an abduction situation. It was during this period when most kids were found. Chloe knew no matter how much Sloanne would hate returning to Aberdeen, she would drop everything and high-tail it back. She had run out of the office, gone home, grabbed a few things and caught the first train smoking out of Penn Station.

As the train sped along on its track, the rain began to fall.

Sloanne stared, trance-like, out the window, blinking as each lightening strike blazed across the sky. While she tried to play out all the possible scenarios in her mind, she rolled her shoulders to relieve the stiffness and tension building in her neck. She ran one hand through her long, auburn hair as she gazed out the window and saw the reflection looking back at her.

Her normally bright, green eyes looked somber and heavy and her clear, pale skin appeared sallow and lifeless. The face that usually smiled back at her, was not smiling now. She wondered if she would ever be happy again. Every ounce of her five-five willowy frame was draped in sadness. She wanted to think that by the time she arrived, Danni would have been found at some boy's house or over at a friend's they'd forgotten to call. She imagined Danni spending an eternity locked in her room, allowed out only for school, bathroom breaks and the occasional meal. A slight grin played across the corners of her mouth as she once again told herself, everything would be just fine and life would continue much as it had before.

She wanted so badly to believe all these things, but could not drown out the sound of that nagging voice in the back of her mind. The voice of reason that kept asking the really tough questions. What if they never found Danni? Or worse, what if her best friend's, precious daughter became another face on a flyer, just another name on a long list of missing and exploited children? Worse still, what if they found her and nothing turned out well? What if everything went horribly wrong and Danni was found raped, injured or dead? She reached up and gently traced Danni's name into the fog on the train window, then leaned back in the seat and closed her eyes, trying to shake the terrible thoughts from her mind.

She thought back to her life in Aberdeen and all she left behind. She had been an average, little girl raised by Irish parents and her family was always very close. Her father and her Uncle Patty—who was actually her godfather—were partners for years on the NYPD: New York's finest. They trained together, worked together and were fast friends. Sloanne knew they had even fallen in love with the same woman...her mom. But her mother had chosen to marry her dad and in the end, Uncle Patty understood her mother's decision. He stepped aside, but remained a true friend to them both. Dad and Uncle Patty moved up through the ranks on the force and both made detective within three months of each other. They worked together then as well. Even when her dad was shot in the line of duty and was forced to retire, Uncle Patty was still there for them all.

He helped out: first, when her parents decided to move to Aberdeen so their little princess could live in a relatively, crime-free environment. Later, when Sloanne was older, he'd been her adult confidante. She remembered begging her dad to teach her to drive and he refused, so afraid she would get hurt. Good old Uncle Patty taught her to drive on the sly and took her for her driving test. Her dad never knew until she came home with her driver's license. Dad put on a big front in the beginning, acting upset with Patty for letting her have her way. She believed that secretly, he had been grateful to Patty. Dad would have been terrified to teach her how to drive himself, this way; Patty saved him from that nightmare. Sloanne smiled to herself at the memory of her father's stern face, but he eventually relented and asked her to drive him to his favorite ice cream parlor. It was then she knew all was well.

Uncle Patty saved the day again when her mom was diagnosed with cancer. He made sure her dad had enough money so it was possible for her mom to receive the finest care available. In a short period, her mother was doing much better and in remission.

As a young girl, she always wanted to live and work in New York City and both, her parents and Uncle Patty, supported her in these hopes. Little had she known in those days, after high school graduation, the desire to live in the city would be overshadowed by her need to be in a drug rehabilitation facility. Those had been her darkest days, but her father and Patty pulled together the love, support and money needed for her to check into the most progressive drug treatment facility in New York. Sloanne never used drugs and was always an excellent student...until she met *him* in her senior year.

His name was Skyler Anthony Perryman, better known around Aberdeen, as Skip. He was the son of the richest and most influential couple in the area, John A. Perryman and his powerhouse wife, Rochelle Ana. He was into banking and investments and she was into real estate. Skip's parents were the epitome of a well-to-do family and owned most of the real estate in and around Aberdeen, along with some of the private docks and marinas on the Susquehanna River and Chesapeake Bay.

Sloanne believed then, that the sun rose and set because of Skip—for a while. Skip attended a private school that cost more per year than most elite colleges. He was a member of the Lacrosse team, the Rugby team captain and probably the most well known person in and around the community with the exception of his father and mother. Skip was also the local drug connection for every man, woman and child with good breeding and a fat bank account in Aberdeen. His friends hated Sloanne for what she was not...rich and he loved her for what she was...not rich.

In the beginning of her relationship with Skip, she told herself he would love her more if she used drugs with him, believing that she would more easily fit into his world by being like his friends, who all used. As time progressed, she managed to convince herself that was the reason she began using drugs.

Luckily, through years of hard work fighting her addiction and facing the reality of it, she now knew it was all about choices. She made the wrong choices. She wanted so badly to fit-in with the high-class crowd Skip ran with, she simply forgot who she was and the things she believed in. Somewhere in loving Skip, she forgot to love herself.

Eventually, it became apparent to everyone, including her parents and the local authorities, that she was routinely testing Skip's drug supply. She became a complicated liability and Skip very quickly left her high and dry. In her family's mind, all that was left to do was for her to get cleaned up and start over fresh in a new town. Her dad, mom and Uncle Patty were her saviors. Her dad worked out the details with some help from Patty and she was soon checked into a nice room in drug rehab in New York City, receiving the help she needed.

The program at the clinic was operated and overseen by Columbia University. Some of the patients there were alumni of the school and were, for whatever reason, discreetly tucked away to handle their problems away from the watchful eyes of their co-workers, peers and families.

One older gentleman there, Philippe Miera, took the time to really listen to her and never judged her. At the end of their six months together, he offered her an internship at his architectural firm with the stipulation, she go back to school and get her degree. So, that's just what she did. She petitioned his Alma Mater, applying for and receiving several grants. To show her how much he believed in her, Mr. Miera paid for her books, fees and all the extras. He also went as far as to pay her a salary that allowed her to live comfortably without having to ask for help from her family. She studied hard and excelled in her school work, while learning the ins and outs of interior design and architecture.

This arrangement was just fine with her parents and Uncle Patty. They knew she needed the structure and socialization that college and a job could provide. They also believed being farther away made it easier to get Skip out of her mind. These facts, along with the added benefit of building a lucrative career with a highly reputable design firm, made this opportunity golden in their eyes. Toss in the fact she was only a two-and-a-half hour train ride from Aberdeen and everything was nearly perfect.

She made every effort, never to go back to Aberdeen for any reason. There was no need to during her college years. Her mom, dad and Patty would either drive up or take the train almost every weekend to visit. On the weekends they couldn't come, Chloe and Danni made the trip as often as possible and they would all 'do' the city.

Now, she thought back to the last day she was in Aberdeen. It was the worst day of her life and one that would live with her forever. Sheets of rain driven by wind pounded the sea of umbrellas and the sad faces of those without any shelter. Two coffins sat, side-by-side, covered with so many flowers it was hard to say what color they were. Beautiful words were spoken by strangers and friends alike and condolences given from lips, quietly whispered with heartfelt hugs.

"We commit these bodies to the ground. Ashes to ashes, dust to dust," the priest's last words. Sloanne's parents were killed in an accident while driving up to see her. It was Uncle Patty who knocked on her door that day and as she saw him standing there alone, she instinctively knew. Her dad, while driving with her mom, lost control of the vehicle, which flipped several times before an eighteen-wheeler slammed into the remains of their car. There wasn't much left, really. It took the rescue crew three hours to extract what they referred to as 'the bodies'. But, they were her parents and she'd never gotten to see them again.

She watched as they'd slowly lowered her mom and dad, one at a time, into the muddy ground. They were there for her beginning and she had been there for their end. There were three people in this world who loved her as their child and she wanted to die as she watched two of them disappear into darkness. Uncle Patty was there to catch her as the first shovel full of dirt was thrown in.

"Don't cover them up! It's dark in there!" she screamed as she dove for their caskets.

But Patty held her back and they both watched and cried as the two best people on earth were buried.

The rest of that day was a blur. People coming and going, bringing food that would never be eaten. Everyone grieved the loss of a wonderful couple. She didn't believe a single person who knew her mom and dad did not love and respect them, and it showed in the number of mourners who came to pay their final respects.

Patty remained close by for months after the funeral. He was her rock and kept her sane in the weeks and months after her parents' deaths. When she returned to the city, he called her constantly, visiting every weekend to make sure she was okay and that her life was getting back on track. They were family and they did the best they could for each other. She tried to be there for him and he helped her to feel loved as a daughter.

Time was winding down now and in fifteen minutes she would be back there. Back where all those feelings and memories lived. The announcement came, "Next stop, Aberdeen Maryland."

She tensed, knowing she could not run away any longer. This time she had to stay and fight. This time she could not break. She had to be strong for Chloe and even stronger for Danni. She whispered a prayer for guidance, then gathered her things and stepped into the aisle.

THREE

Arrival

Passengers began to move about, gathering their belongings, as the train slowed to a stop at the station. Most wore big smiles or chatted away, their excitement obvious, but Sloanne's face was shrouded in terror. Her nails bit into the palms of her clenched hand and she felt certain she must be the only person there who carried such disdain for Aberdeen Maryland.

She leaned down to peer through the grimy train window at her Uncle Patty who was standing on the platform, hands folded in front of him, waiting for her to arrive. He was smiling at her. He knew she needed to see that; to feel that comfort and she smiled back because she knew he deserved as much. Inside, Sloanne was an emotional wreck. The outside wasn't much better. Her hands were trembling and she tried to ignore them as she grabbed her bags, but nearly dropped them. Nausea began to rise in her stomach causing her mouth to water. She swallowed hard, willing herself to be calm, as the first beads of sweat became visible on her forehead.

"Ma'am, are you all right? You look a bit pale," an older gentleman asked as he lightly touched her shoulder.

"Thank you. I am fine, probably just something I ate."

She did her very best to sound convincing as the man gave her a kind smile and made his way off the train.

Sloanne shut her eyes tight and took a deep breath, then began to ease gingerly down the isle. She had come here for one purpose, to help Chloe find her daughter. She refocused and stepped off the train right into the open arms of her loving godfather.

"Oh I've missed you, kiddo." he said as he hugged her and Sloanne could find no words to respond.

She simply hugged him back and that seemed to be enough for him. Long seconds passed before the gravity of the situation hit her. She was safe in his arms as she surrendered to the uncontrollable tears that began to fall from her eyes. She missed him more than she knew and hated the fact they lived so far apart. He was her home, her security in the world; he was all the family she had left.

"Don't cry, kiddo," Patty said soothingly.

He reached up and held her face in his hands as he smoothed away the tears from her cheeks.

"I have missed you too."

His words told her that Patty knew exactly what was in her heart and that he felt the same.

"Here, let me take your bags. I have my car waiting out front and I'm double-parked. We should try to hurry."

"What should I expect?" she asked with uncertainty in her voice, "I don't want to be caught off guard."

"You can expect to see a lot of police cars, there will be detectives asking questions and a lot of coming and going. They are planning and organizing search parties as we speak and with that comes volunteers as well. People want to help, Sloanne."

Patty's voice was sincere as he looked at her. There was also something else in his eyes, something guarded that Sloanne picked up on.

"What are you not telling me?"

With a sudden change in demeanor, Patty angrily said, "Those damned Perryman's will be there. They have offered all their resources and under the circumstances, the police felt compelled to take them up on their offer. You know anytime something happens in Aberdeen, they are right there in the middle of it. That Rochelle is a piece of work, always advertising that damned, Real Estate Company and John isn't much better. He lets her get away with whatever. If he knew what people around here really think of his pansy-ass, he'd cut that woman off at the knees."

"Shit. I knew it. I knew I couldn't get through this without seeing them, but I didn't think I would have to deal with them this soon."

Sloanne's eyes looked away as she let out a labored sigh.

"I don't like it either and I am sorry, Sloanne. The police are doing everything they can in this situation. I have asked that Skip stay away and the Perryman's agreed that it would be best, so you won't have that to worry about that."

Patty shuffled his feet and lightly kicked a rock that lay on the ground as he spoke.

"I appreciate that Patty, but it doesn't make me any more anxious to get there," Sloanne's exaggerated laugh trailed off at the end of her words.

She saw the guilt on his face as he looked at her. She knew this was for the best and they needed all the help they could get finding Danni. She reached out and squeezed his arm,

"Don't worry. I'll be fine, really."

"That's my girl," he said with a warm smile

"We should go then."

"After you," he replied.

The two climbed into Patty's car and headed in the direction of Chloe's house.

Everything looked exactly the way Sloanne remembered it. Nothing ever seemed to change in small towns. Aberdeen was no exception. She watched the scenery slip by through the window, taking notice of newly painted storefronts and fresh asphalt. Images flashed like old photographs through Sloanne's mind of good and bad times in the small town she once called home. She reached up, unaware and ran a nervous hand through her hair. Sensing her unease, Patty reached over and took her hand in his. Without saying a word, he gave her hand a light squeeze and Sloanne smiled.

As soon as they made the turn into Chloe's neighborhood, the air seemed to change and the tension could be felt. There was law enforcement everywhere. The normally quiet, peaceful, residential neighborhood with the birch-lined streets and beautiful flower beds over-flowing with every color on earth was now completely obscured by cars that filled the street as far as the eye could see. People were scattered about on both sides of the street. There were strangers and some news crews, but many Sloanne had known since her childhood.

Sloanne spotted the balding, lanky figure of Aberdeen's local news vulture, Mr. Birney Sullivan, standing alone on one side of the yard.

"Great…how long has he been here?" Sloanne gestured with a nod of her head in the reporter's direction.

Patty looked up and with a half smile said, "What, are you kidding? He was the first one here."

Birney Sullivan had been with the *Aberdeen Chronicle* for years and everyone in the county knew him. He had an 'in your face' approach to journalism few had patience for. He was the unrelenting face and voice of every crime that ever took place in Aberdeen or Harford County, Maryland. With his signature pair of glasses shoved up on his forehead and a camera slung around his neck, he looked like a tall, aging Jimmy Olsen from a *Superman* comic. Most considered Birney a snake on two legs and felt he had no respect for the decent people in the area. An abduction story was big news and Sloanne knew Birney would sop up every ounce of it he could. She

43

didn't know Birney Sullivan personally, but she was sure she didn't want to either.

Sloanne continued to scan the faces of those lining the street when she caught site of Mr. and Mrs. Perryman. She chuckled just a bit to herself when she saw them. They looked so out of place on the front lawn of Chloe's modest home. John Perryman was of average height and had an athletic, but aging build with a shortish, spiky hair cut and round, gold-rimmed glasses. Even in this casual environment, he seemed a little too well dressed.

Rochelle Perryman was right by his side, looking like she'd just stepped off the cover of a magazine: medium height, nicely built, with strawberry-blond hair, cut in a fashionable style and very blue eyes fringed with long, beautiful lashes. Immaculately dressed in what Sloanne was sure Rochelle would consider casual attire. Rochelle Perryman stood out from everyone around her. It looked as if they were holding court and some of the people were hanging around them simply because of who they are. Sloanne shook her head at how ridiculous it seemed.

Most people were in shock over something like this happening in a town like Aberdeen and each one wanted to do all they could to help.

Sloanne and Patty pulled up to the house as close as possible and stepped out. As they drew closer to the house, they could see a staging area for the search parties. A large canopy had been erected and tables filled with Gatorade, bottled water and maps, sat underneath. A dozen maps were laid end to end while people gathered around planning their tracking routes.

The voices all droned together making it difficult for Sloanne to concentrate. She tugged nervously at her clothing as she walked towards the front door of her best friend's home. Dread lay heavy in the back of her mind as she steadied herself for Chloe's reaction. With a nervous sigh, Sloanne continued through the yard and up to the front steps.

Just as she was about to place a foot onto Chloe's front porch, Rochelle Perryman touched her arm to gain her attention causing Sloanne to stop dead in her tracks.

"Sloanne, it's been such a long time. You look wonderful and I hear you're doing quite well at your firm in New York," she said, without any hint of pleasure in her voice. "John and I were just saying how well you've made out since your parents' deaths. Who would have thought that *you* would ever have made such a lucrative place for yourself in the world?"

"Well hello, Rochelle. I see you're looking completely out of place, as usual."

Sloanne's response was quick and blunt. There was once a time when this woman could reduce her to an inarticulate idiot with very few words, but that time had come and gone. They never liked one another and it was apparent to all the people within earshot.

Rochelle felt Sloanne was intruding on 'her' town by being here, but she could not have cared less.

"Sloanne?" Rochelle's voice dropped to a whisper, "I can't say that I was ever fond of you or that I think it is a good idea, but my son asked me to tell you that he wants to see you while you're in town. It goes against my better judgment to relay this message to you, but you know I would do anything for my Skip. Even something I *don't* agree with."

"I am well aware of exactly what you'd do for your Skip. Rochelle, is there anything else you need to say to me?"

Sloanne longed to reach out and knock Rochelle Perryman on her fancy ass.

"There's nothing more, Sloanne." Rochelle's pretty head seemed to spin around until out popped that sweet, concerned side that said, "Please relay our sympathies to Chloe. We are all so concerned about young Danni and we will do whatever it takes to bring her home."

How did she do that? Act so much like she cared for anyone other that her fancy friends and well-to-do family. It was something Sloanne had never been able to understand about people like Rochelle. It was amazing to her how fake this woman could be. *Who the hell did she think she was and who would stoop to pimping out their only son at a time like this*? The questions popped into Sloanne's head, but she thought better of asking them and simply turned away in disgust and made her way inside.

As she entered the house, Chloe ran to her.

"Oh Sloanne…my baby is gone."

Chloe wrapped her arms around Sloanne and the two women clung tightly to each other as the tears rolled down.

Sloanne felt helpless as her friend nearly collapsed at her side. She held Chloe up and helped her over to the sofa. She loved Danni like her own, but still could not fathom what Chloe was going through. She did not know what it was to give birth to a little girl whom she raised and cared for all her life. She had no idea what it was like to stay up all night with a sick child. She had never known the first day of school or given comfort after a nightmare.

Sloanne knew she loved Danni dearly, but it was not the same as being her mother. She knew Chloe would never give up on Danni being found and now she knew she never would either. She would never give up, never let go, never stop until Danni was found.

The two sat very close on the sofa and Sloanne cradled Chloe as they both cried. Chloe had her cell in one hand and the house phone within arms' reach. Pictures of Danni were spread all over the coffee table and photo albums were lying scattered on the floor. There were two gentlemen leaned over the end table setting up a digital voice/telephone recording device that would intercept and record any calls and trace the number from any possible kidnappers.

Some of the neighborhood ladies were in Chloe's kitchen

making coffee and preparing plates of food for the officers and searchers from the many dishes that had been sent over by a caring community. There was also a group of men standing in one corner Sloanne figured had to be detectives from the local police station. She was not sure what to say next, but knew Chloe was looking to her for strength.

Patty strode in through the front door and approached the group of officers.

"Get me up to speed on where we are? Have we gotten any hits from the *Amber Alert* yet?"

His voice was strong and commanding.

Though Patty was no longer on the police force full-time, he still consulted for them and owned a small security firm of his own. He was well respected by the members of the police community. He knew most of the detectives and there was mutual cooperation and respect amongst them all. He supplied most of the technical equipment used by the force in and around the area and was friendly with the guys on and off duty.

One of the men, a detective, came forward and said, "We have a BOLO issued for the entire state of Maryland. We haven't gotten any hits on the *Amber Alert* so far. There have been no calls from outside the home other than the usual inquiries as to the state of the investigation. I've got our guy working on the skid marks from the back lot of the grocery, but it is looking like they were too blurred to tell us much. He did indicate that the tracks looked to be from a foreign-made tire and probably a brand which would be used on a smaller, sporty model vehicle. That's about all we have at this point. We're trying to keep this investigation in-house for now, but the state people have been notified and have offered their resources in the event we decide we need them."

"That's not much considering we're already six hours into this," Patty said incredulously.

The look on his face was hard to discern.

"Do you have any idea why someone would take Danni? I mean, have there been any other abductions in this area or is this an M.O. you guys have seen around here before?" Sloanne asked.

Her question seemed to come from nowhere, but she was from a 'police family' and picked up a lot of the jargon in her youth. It was something that always stuck with the kid of a cop.

The other men in the room stopped and gave her a surprised look, but just as quickly seemed to settle back into the knowledge that she was the product of a law enforcement upbringing. These men all knew who her father was and that fact, made Sloanne family for them.

The detective, who was the mouthpiece of the group said, "Ms Kelly, we have never had this type of crime happen around here and we are at a loss to link this to any previous crimes in the area. We have so little experience with this kind of thing here. We're really just winging it."

"Winging It? Where the hell were *you* trained in police work?" Patty nearly screamed at the man.

Sloanne read the look on Patty's stern face. She knew he was on edge, but it was not like him to lose his cool.

"Sorry, Mr. Louchlin, but I personally have never worked this kind of case before and very few of these other guys have either. Most of these men are going into overtime on this case and we are doing all we can. If you have any suggestions on what else we could be doing, please feel free to throw them out there. We have put out feelers to all the surrounding precincts and I personally have spoken to the state police. They are checking as to any other crimes of this nature in the immediate area and will get back to us if they come up with anything. In the meantime, we are organizing as many search parties as we have manpower to cover and making up flyers to spread around the county. We've got men working the phones and we're about as up to speed as we can be," the detective stared at Patty as he spoke, but dropped his eyes as his words trailed off.

Sloanne could see by the look in Patty's eyes that he knew these men were doing as much as possible and she watched as he mentally went over all his training, making sure there was nothing going undone. She recognized something else there in his eyes too, something she could never recall seeing before. It was more a look of uncertainty and not something that Sloanne generally associated with Patty's usual demeanor. She knew he was worried about Danni and Chloe and about her.

She could only look away.

FOUR

Chloe

Chloe and Sloanne met only hours after Sloanne's family arrived in Aberdeen. In fact, Chloe was the first person Sloanne laid eyes on in her new town. She'd slept through the car ride down and woke up in her own room in their new home.

When the decision to move had been made by her parents, she'd known very little about where they would be moving. Only that it was a small town in Maryland with good schools and a low crime rate. She remembered her dad telling her about Aberdeen. They were talking about the move and her dad was trying to make her understand why they were leaving New York in the first place. She was already old enough to be in a school she liked and was familiar with her neighborhood. She didn't want to leave there, mostly because this home contained the friends she went to school with and were close to for as long as she'd been old enough to have friends.

Sloanne remembered being very sad about leaving behind everything she'd grown up with her entire life. She also remembered Uncle Patty telling her, home was not a place you lived, but a place where your heart lived.

She tried, for her parents and Patty, to do as he asked, but her heart just wasn't in it...until she met Chloe.

CRUELTY TO INNOCENTS

Chloe lived down the street from her new house and was the first kid Sloanne saw on her maiden venture outside. Chloe was walking past Sloanne's front yard, heading to school. Sloanne was easily able to tell that the little girl was curious about the new kid on the block. Sloanne remembered smiling to herself at the sight of Chloe walking and secretly trying to catch a glimpse of the new girl that moved into the neighborhood.

The neighborhood school Chloe attended and that she would also be going to, was just a couple blocks up and over from their neighborhood and Sloanne's mom was driving her there for her first day.

Her mom and dad met Chloe's parents previous to the move and her mom recognized Chloe as she passed that day, calling out to her to see if she wanted to ride along with them.

"Sure, that would be great," Chloe said in her quiet, small voice as she approached the car. Sloanne thought how beautiful Chloe was, with her long, blond hair and cornflower, blue eyes, just like a fairy princess. She never liked her own, more Irish look; dark hair with that tint of auburn and green eyes. Her collection of Barbie dolls contained only those with blond hair and she always wished she could be so pretty and fairy-like.

When Chloe jumped into the back seat of her mom's car that day, the first thing she said to Sloanne was, 'You have the most beautiful colored hair and pretty eyes, just like a fairy princess.'

Sloanne fell instantly in love with Chloe.

Needless to say, from that day on, Chloe and Sloanne were best friends. They were both in the same, third grade class at school. They loved riding bikes together and building forts in the woods behind their homes. They played 'cops and robbers' together with some of the other neighborhood kids. Of course, Sloanne was always a cop and Chloe never seemed to mind being the bad guy. They both became Girl Scouts together and even started noticing boys at the same time. They'd get together and write little skits that all the neighborhood kids would participate in and all the parents would attend, right in their back yards. Their parents always got together at birthday time and celebrated with a joint birthday party because the girls' birthdays were only two days apart.

Chloe and Sloanne always said they were really sisters, but with different parents. They would talk for hours about what they would be when they grew up and how they'd move away to California together; Chloe to be a movie star and Sloanne to be in a rock band.

During their junior year in high school, Chloe fell madly in love with a guy whose dad owned the local garage. Joe Jacobs was a good looking kid, but Sloanne never felt he really cared about Chloe the way she deserved. Sloanne was all into Skip at that time, so the two girls didn't run in the same crowd, but Chloe and Sloanne would still talk on the phone, spend the night together and discuss their dreams. Those dreams changed quite a bit from their childhood and now that they were older, all Chloe wanted was to marry Joe and raise a house full of kids. A few months before graduation, Chloe realized she was pregnant and that led to the inevitable shotgun wedding between her and Joe.

By this time, Sloanne was into Skip's drugs so heavy she was not there for Chloe and when Danni was born, Sloanne was already in rehab.

Chloe never held it against Sloanne. Besides the fact she let her parents and Patty down so badly; letting Chloe down was one of the worst things Sloanne felt she had done in her life. Chloe was always there for her and visited her in rehab when Joe would allow it, which wasn't often. Sloanne believed things must have gotten pretty hard for Chloe in those years after she left Aberdeen. They would write and talk on the phone occasionally, but Chloe never seemed like the same happy, free-spirited girl Sloanne was so close to. Later, she found out through her mom that Joe abused Chloe quite a bit during their marriage and she was so ashamed, she never could bring herself to tell Sloanne. Chloe confided to Sloanne's mom that she worried Joe would eventually hurt Danni and she planned many times to leave him, but was afraid.

Finally, one day, Joe left Chloe and Danni and never came back. To say their lives changed drastically, was putting it mildly.

Chloe enrolled at the area, technical school and received a

certificate that helped her land a job as a receptionist with one of the local, medical clinics. She had a chance to make a life for herself and Danni, without the fear of it all being snatched away by a demanding husband. Everything in their lives got better.

Now, Chloe lost the only thing in her life that really made sense—her daughter. They were both devastated. Some fairy tale their lives turned out to be. Sitting there with Chloe, Sloanne thought about how innocent they both were then; how naive and trusting. Seeing the way things were now made Sloanne want to cry. How differently their lives turned out, unlike anything they could have foreseen in past days. All those sweet, child-like notions were little more than fading dreams and the real world was taking hold and crashing down, hard and fast.

The first search parties were gone and some of the people in Chloe's home thinned out. Chloe and Sloanne were finally able to talk freely.

"How are you really doing?" Sloanne asked Chloe, feeling certain she already knew the answer.

She'd never stopped crying since Sloanne walked in the door and now the tears began to fall in a fresh wave.

"You raise a child and nurture that child and love them with everything you have and never once stop to think that one day they may disappear from your life," she said between sobs. "I've seen flyers for missing kids before, but I never thought that could happen to Danni. What if they never find her? How can I go from having my sweet, baby girl here this morning, to not knowing where she is or if I will ever see her again, in one, short day?"

The pain in Chloe's eyes was almost too much for Sloanne to bear. She knew she must tell her friend something that would make her have hope that Danni would be found.

"Listen Chloe, I know how much Danni means to you. I love her like she is my own and we both must have faith that she will be found safe and well and will be back here with us very soon. Patty and the police are doing everything they can and I'm certain that Danni is okay."

Even as Sloanne said the words to Chloe, she could only hope they were true. This had to be the way the situation played out and she prayed Danni would be found quickly. Chloe looked so dragged out and hollow and Sloanne wanted to try to get her mind working in another direction.

"How long has it been since you've eaten?" Sloanne asked her friend.

"I don't know. This morning maybe," Chloe tiredly replied.

"Maybe we should think about getting some food in you. When Danni gets home, you'll have to be there for her and you can't do that without food and rest," Sloanne prodded.

"I just don't think I can eat," Chloe breathed a choked sigh.

"I don't want to hear that. I'm going to fix you something

and I want you to stretch out on this sofa and rest while I'm in the kitchen," Sloanne stood with her hands fisted on her hips.

Chloe relented and Sloanne knew the woman had to be bone-tired to do so. She covered her friend with a throw from the back of the sofa and headed to the kitchen to see what she could find.

As she entered the kitchen, Sloanne thought about Danni. *Where could she be? Is she hungry? Is she cold? Is she scared? What is she going through?* All these things flashed through Sloanne's head and she had to drag herself back to the task at hand. She checked the cabinets, but Chloe was certainly running short on food and she made a mental note to go to the grocery store first thing in the morning, knowing with all that was taking place, there would be extra people to feed.

Next, she checked the fridge. There were still a few sandwiches on a tray so she took a couple out and placed them, along with some chips, on a plate for Chloe. She grabbed a couple of Diet Cokes and some glasses and then made her way back to the front room. As Chloe came into view, she could see that sleep finally claimed her, but it was not a peaceful sleep. Chloe's mouth twitched a few times as if she was about to speak or cry out and Sloanne could see her hands gripping her cell tightly. She set the plate of food down and turned out the lamp behind Chloe's head, then settled herself into the over-stuffed chair beside the sofa. She heard the back door creak as one of the remaining officers came into the kitchen to refill his cup from the coffee pot on the counter. He then peeked around the door to check on Chloe and saw her sleeping on the sofa as Sloanne rested in the chair. A slight smile crossed his lips and he backed away to leave the same way he entered.

Sloanne was starting to feel the effects of the last twenty four hours and it wasn't long before she was fitfully dreaming of eerie shadows and hearing a child crying in the darkness.

FIVE

Collide

George and Martha Hendrix were a loving couple, but with any couple who spent fifty-two years staring at one another, day in and day out, also came some conflict. They loved one another, but if there was one thing in all their years of wedded bliss that could start an argument—it was George's driving!

"You pulled out right in front of that man, George, you damn idiot," Martha bellowed from the passenger seat, her small wrinkled frame barely visible over the dashboard. "I tell you George Hendrix, you will be the death of me yet."

"Oh there you go again: nag, nag, nag. I get so tired of it, woman. I should have left you at home when you asked to come. You would think after fifty-two years of listening to the same old nagging, I would know better than to even bring you along," George retorted as he returned a spitfire glare in Martha's direction.

The fireworks really began then, as was usually the case.

"Why George Hendrix, you mean old shit, you know good and well I didn't ask to come. You asked me, more than once."

Martha sat up high in her seat. She was flaming mad now and the battle was really on.

"Like I said, you would think after all these years, I would have better sense than to take you anywhere." George's answer came swift and loud. He continued, "I have never wrecked us before have I?" George screamed into the windshield, never taking his eyes from the road. "Well have I?"

Martha leaned over close to George's ear and grit her false teeth as she answered.

"No, but the day is still young and we haven't made it home yet."

Martha used the same line every time the argument over George's driving popped up and today was no exception. Some things in life you could always count on to remain a constant. One was that George's driving was never going to get any better and the other…Martha was never going to stop reminding him of that fact. George and Martha neared the second of two stops they needed to make before heading back home.

The last stop was the pharmacy to pick up George's blood pressure medicine he had been taking for quite a few years. To hear him tell it, this was due to the fact that Martha's cooking was too fattening and she rode him too hard about petty things, such as his driving. All these things caused him undue stress and naturally…high blood pressure. Of course no one could say for sure. His doctor did say, on more than one occasion, it could be something as simple as heredity. But to George, this was just not possible, even though his brother died three years prior of a heart attack. No, to hear

George Hendrix tell it, heredity was just an excuse doctors used when they didn't know what was wrong with you. If ol' George had high blood pressure, then it could be no other than Martha Hendrix who was to blame. After all, they had been married for fifty-two years and no matter who you are or how healthy you seem, fifty-two years with the same woman was bound to run anyone's blood pressure sky high.

"Now Martha, I don't want to hear another word about it. I have to pick up this prescription and then I'll get you straight home."

When George used this tone of voice with Martha, she pretty much knew to end the conversation, but not today. Today, Martha had been determined to say her piece and today she did.

"George Hendrix, I have had all I am going to take from you today or any day. You think because I have listened to you for a lifetime that makes you right and me wrong. Well, let me tell you a thing or two, mister. I am not wrong, you are not right and I will not wait until you pick up a single thing. You will take me home now, not later or so help me George, you will not have another moment's peace for the rest of your miserable life. Better yet, pull this car over right this minute, George Hendrix. I won't ride another mile with your driving."

Martha was at her wits end and the glare from her squinted eyes told him so.

The look on George's face was priceless and Martha couldn't

help but smile a little on the inside. George turned and stared at Martha with mouth agape, shocked at what she said.

He could only bring himself to say one word, "Sorry."

That's when everything went from bad to worse. George was looking at Martha instead of the road—as usual—and missed seeing the red light at one of the busiest intersections in Aberdeen. Mr. and Mrs. George Hendrix just had the final argument of their married lives.

SIX

Fortuity

Sloanne walked out of the grocery store and placed all her purchases in the back seat of Chloe's car. Slamming the back door, she turned to get in the front and leave when she heard it. The sounds were like something from a movie: tires locking up and skidding on asphalt, a horn blaring so loudly and then that slamming, screeching, crunching, metal-on-metal sound of a horrendous car crash not eighty feet away from her in the intersection of Aberdeen's two main thoroughfares. All this happened in a split second and as she looked up, her heart froze in her chest and she stopped breathing momentarily. Strange shades of long ago memories flew through her head as she looked on the gruesome site and her parents' faces jumped into her minds eye.

The driver of the big, silver fuel truck never saw the car driven by George Hendrix until it was directly in front of him, leaving him little opportunity to avoid the collision. The huge truck ripped into the Buick's, passenger-side door with the force of a missile and the car completely folded into the truck's front grill. The momentum of the fuel truck impacting with the mid-sized car dragged it along, but only until it crumpled against the very large, old-fashioned, wooden, power pole causing the car to be sandwiched between the truck and the pole with a bone-crunching, ear-splitting

64

crack. The trailer of the rig jack-knifed around to form an 'L', with the rear end sticking out, blocking one lane of traffic.

Sloanne took all of this in, but the only thing her mind could think was, *Mom and Dad...I have to help them,* and she found herself running towards the terrible disaster before she realized the danger. She could hear someone screaming and the sounds of running behind her. Other people in the grocery store had also seen what was happening and someone immediately called 9-1-1.

The driver of the truck was the first one out of his cab. Bleeding profusely from a cut on his forehead, he had not really stepped out of his truck as much as fallen out. He dragged himself up and limped to the front of his truck praying he would find the passengers alive. The Hendrix's Buick hardly resembled a car at all. The truck driver took one look, turned, doubled over and vomited in the grass beside the highway. He had seen carnage in his life, but never anything like this and he nearly fainted from the site. As Sloanne ran up to the man, tears were streaming down his face and the look in his eyes was like nothing she'd ever witnessed. He seemed to be aware, but there was no light left there at all. She helped the driver move a safe distance away from the twisted wreckage. As she helped the man sit down in the grass, she saw a large, bloody gash in his left pant leg that was pumping fresh blood at an alarming rate. Sloanne pulled the scarf from around her neck and quickly wrapped it around the man's leg and then placed his own hand on it, telling him to hold tightly.

Sloanne smelled smoke as she saw flames lapping at the dashboard and front hood of the Hendrixs' vehicle. She ran back towards the wreckage to see if she could help the passengers escape. She saw Martha Hendrix's broken, crumpled body, still strapped into the passenger seat. Martha had been killed instantly from the blunt force of the impact. As Sloanne neared, she could see the old man in the driver's seat. George Hendrix had sustained major injuries to his left arm, which was now twisted and gnarled from the impact. Sloanne shuddered and squeezed her eyes shut for a split second when she saw the old man's gaping head wound. He was alive and he was begging for his wife to forgive him.

"Come on Martha, I'll let you drive from now on...Please, Martha."

Over and over the words came with no reply. Sloanne thought to herself, *How could he be alive? How could he still be talking?*

"Sir...please, sir, let me help you," Sloanne calmly said to the old man.

She could feel the intense heat from the flames that leapt from the car. She reached out in an attempt to touch the old man's shoulder when two, large, strong arms grabbed Sloanne from behind and literally lifted her away from where she'd been standing next to the old man in the car. It happened so quickly she didn't realize what was going on until she was placed back on the ground some distance from where she'd previously been. The shock left her standing there with her mouth open, watching the broad back of a retreating fireman with *AFD* and a big *#5* blazoned across it. The man was now headed back to assist the accident victims. She never even heard the fire truck arriving.

Sloanne watched as the flames overtook the interior of the Buick. Firefighters began to douse the flames, trying in vain, to save the passengers. It was then that she realized the severity of the situation she had just been removed from. It was as if she was possessed and her body just ran out into the middle of the hellish scene with no idea of how dangerous the situation really was. All she thought was she needed to help.

She watched a large, bucket truck with *Maryland Power Association* written on the cab door and lights flashing on top pull up in the middle of the street just down from the carnage. Two guys jumped out and immediately started to work. One man jumped up on the back of the truck and into the bucket, while the other started it up towards a transformer at the top of a pole about three lengths down from the one that was now leaning over the top of the fuel truck. They were trying to cut the power so the firemen and EMTs could get to the mangled car. The driver of the fuel truck was now on a gurney a good way from his vehicle and was being lifted into the back of a waiting ambulance. As the power crew cut the power, the firemen continued to foam down the street. Two police cars, also with lights flashing, pulled up and were angled across two other streets that formed the intersection to keep anyone else from inadvertently driving through the accident scene. The fire truck was angled across the remaining street, effectively forming a barrier at all four points of the intersection.

She noticed the gathering crowd and the news van that skidded into the grocery store parking lot. She also noticed Birney Sullivan exit, almost slink in fact, from the van and run towards the scene with his camera up and ready to start clicking off pictures as soon as he got close enough to get good shots of the gore. *What a despicable man he is*, she thought. Sloanne knew people within the reaches of the *Aberdeen Chronicle* wanted to know the news and of course, read about everything that was going on in the world. But Birney had a way of turning every bit of news he reported on into some sort of sleazy nastiness that only the lowest of fans wanted to be a part of. He just had that way about him and Sloanne never understood why the news editor kept Birney on at the paper. But, there he was, clicking away at everything he could get close to. Right up in the firemens way, doing his thing. It seemed so disrespectful. One of the firemen even yelled at him to get back and when Birney ignored him, the fireman grabbed him around the arm and bodily guided him away from the pitiful bodies of the victims. Sloanne noticed it was the same fireman who forcibly disengaged her from amidst the wreckage earlier. She wondered if this was part of his assigned tasks as a fireman or if he just didn't like people getting in his way.

Sloanne stood there watching the organized chaos, unable to pull herself away from the scene in front of her. She had never been so close to a dying person and she sadly wondered if anyone was there the day her parents died. Had anyone tried to help them? Had any passer-by stopped and offered a hand to either of them as they lay in the wreckage of their car? She didn't know. All she knew was, even though it had been foolish of her to run into the mangled midst of the crash, she hoped someone had done the same for her parents.

She stood there for a long time, lost in her thoughts and feeling torn up over the old couple who lost their lives there today. She wondered if they had kids who would miss them, as she missed her parents. She wondered if they had been happy in their lives. She wondered why things like this happened to anyone.

Just then, she felt someone place a hand on her shoulder very softly. It didn't startle her at all because of the lightness of the touch. As she turned around, she looked up into the most expressive, blue-gray eyes she'd ever seen. She couldn't help but stare.

"I'm sorry I accosted you earlier Sloanne, but you were standing in a very volatile place. I figured the quicker I got you out of there the better. I didn't hurt you, did I?" the fireman asked her with a quirky, half-smile.

"Excuse me, but do I know you?" Sloanne stammered.

"Well, you may not remember me, but I'm Shawn Tyler. We had a few classes together in high school. Remember? You haven't changed a bit. Still pretty as ever," he said his face in a big grin now.

Shawn's face clicked in her memory and she couldn't help but smile back at him.

"Sure, of course. I remember you now, but I can hardly say that you haven't changed since school. I never would have recognized you. You were kind of short and skinny back in those days. But, well, you certainly have filled out," she said embarrassingly.

She kept trying to shut up, but while her mouth was in gear, her brain definitely was not.

She remembered Shawn as a very gangly, short, boy who was rather shy and introverted and something of a book worm. She never really paid much attention to him in school. She found it hard to imagine this tall, well-built man with wavy, light-brown hair, beautiful, blue eyes and ruggedly handsome face was actually that same scrawny kid who'd been in her class. Wow, time certainly did change people.

"I'm sorry if I got in your way out there, but I kind of zoned out when I saw the wreck. It reminded me of…" Sloanne was trying to think as she talked, but she was still seeing her parents and it was difficult to make sense.

"Reminded you of your parents? I'm sorry you had to go through this. I heard about them and I'm real sorry for your loss, Sloanne," Shawn said to her, a bit of sadness playing at the corners of his mouth.

"It's okay. I should be over it by now, but this awful scene makes me think, well…" Sloanne tried to convey her feelings, then wondered why she wanted this man to know how she felt.

"Damn it," Shawn huffed.

Sloanne looked up surprised, but then noticed he was looking towards the wrecked fuel truck. As she turned to see what he was looking at, her eyes fell on Birney, standing there arguing with another of the firemen.

"What a snake that guy is. He has absolutely no respect for anyone, not even the dead," Shawn said with malice in his voice.

"I've said the same thing many times and I'll never understand why the paper keeps that slug around," Sloanne said. "He was all over the search parties and police last night at my friend's house."

"Oh yeah? Chloe Jacobs, right? I remember you two were best friends in school and I heard about her daughter being missing. Bad thing. I think the off-duty crew from my firehouse is helping in the search. Will you tell Chloe I'll be praying for her and her daughter? I'll get by there after my shift to help out. Maybe I'll see you there?" Shawn said now with more of that half-smile showing.

"Thank you Shawn. We appreciate everything being done. Danni is like a daughter to me and I'm really worried about her and Chloe. I can barely think about Danni out there alone. I don't know what will happen if she's not found. I think it will kill Chloe and…"

"Don't even go there, Sloanne. Danni will be found and everything will be fine. Have faith…okay. I've got to go, but I'll be around in a day or so. You keep that pretty chin up," he said with that same big grin and Sloanne had to grin back.

His smile was simply infectious and she couldn't help herself.

Shawn trotted off towards the fire truck and with a final look at the wreckage in the intersection, Sloanne turned to leave.

SEVEN

Blaze

Ed and Gwen Tyler, along with their twin girls, Kimmi and Kammi and their six month old son Aiden, where heading home from the First Baptist Church of Aberdeen. Wednesday night Pot Luck dinner had been the usual family affair for a very long time and one the Tylers always attended. The adults would fellowship and talk about things that needed to be done in the church or the community, while the kids played and sang songs and listened to stories told by the youth minister. Tonight was just like any other Wednesday night supper, nothing unusual. Nine-year-old Kimmi and Kammi continued to sing in the back seat of the Tyler's mini-van, while little Aiden slept in his car seat behind Dad on the seat next to them.

"Gwen, I just don't think we can afford to buy a new refrigerator right now, not with the bills from Aiden's surgery still unpaid."

Ed spoke as the tune of 'Jesus Loves Me' nearly drowned him out from the back seat. He was a big man, about six-four with a stocky build and receding hairline. He always had a pleasant look on his face and was always there for anyone who needed help. He was a good provider, a family man and he loved his wife and kids dearly.

"I know, Ed. I guess we can make do with the one we have for now, but I hate to see you have to keep working on it every time

73

it gives out." Gwen replied.

Gwen Tyler was a small, petite woman with dark hair. Most people thought Ed and Gwen looked odd together because of the difference in their height, but when they met, it had taken only one look for them to realize they found 'the one'. They had been together ever since. Ed often remarked he felt like a giant in his household full of small women, but the birth of little Aiden gave him hope that someday, he would have another tall person in the family.

"Well, sweetheart, Shawn said he'd try to come by and take a look at it first chance he gets and you know he's better at fixing stuff than I am," Ed remarked.

Gwen could only smile as she remembered the last time her husband tried to fix an electrical appliance in their home. That old stove was still sitting in the shed with the burn marks, so obvious, across its front.

"When did you hear from Shawn? How is 'baby brother' these days?"

Ed's brother Shawn was a part of their family and Gwen loved him as if he were her own flesh and blood and not just her brother-in-law.

The blond, blue-eyed twins in the back seat were still singing and paying no mind to their parents' conversation. They loved Wednesday night church suppers because they always got to showcase their singing skills and to them, there was nothing more

74

entertaining.

As they pulled up to the stop sign at an intersection a couple blocks from their home, one of the girls said in a sing-song manner, "Mommy, I think Aiden is waking up."

Ed and Gwen simultaneously turned their heads to look at their children in the back seat.

Wham! The startling sound came from the driver's side window as a hand slapped the glass, jolting them all out of their focus. Everyone in the car jumped and the two little girls squealed aloud. Ed quickly turned to see a shriveled old woman leaning on a walker babbling to his window. He opened his door quickly and she nearly fell into the van.

"Please help my husband! The house is on fire and he's still in there. He can't get out. He's disabled and bed-ridden. I can't get him! Please help me," the old woman frantically screamed as she tugged at Ed's shirt trying to convey the urgency.

Ed threw the van into park and slid out of the driver's seat.

Breaking into a run, he yelled back over his shoulder to his wife, "Call 9-1-1."

Gwen picked up her cell and dialed the number while climbing from the passenger's seat to the driver's side in one, swift movement. She pulled the van through the intersection and parked on the right, just in front of the house that sat diagonally across the street from where the old couple's house was burning.

"9-1-1...what is your emergency?" The operator on the other end asked quickly.

"There is a house fire and a man is trapped inside. We need help," Gwen relayed to the operator.

"Ma'am, can you give me the location?"

Gwen gave the operator the street names at the intersection and the name on the mailbox in front of the burning home, "Welch".

"Ma'am, what is your name?"

Gwen replied with the information.

"I'm dispatching fire and rescue personnel right now. They should arrive there shortly. Would you please remain on the line until..."

It was then that Gwen looked towards the house and saw the old woman starting to go down. She saw the first flames appear over the roof of the house. She dropped her phone and turned to the back seat.

"Is Daddy going to help the lady, Momma," asked the twins, almost in unison.

"Yes, babies...Daddy is going to help. Now I want you two to stay put and don't move. Mommy is going to help the lady. I want you girls to sing to your brother so he doesn't wake up. I'll be back in just a minute, okay?"

The girls happily began to sing as Gwen slipped from the van. She could hear 'Jesus Loves Me' from behind her as she ran to the old woman, who now lay crumpled at the street curb.

Gwen knelt to help the elderly lady, but Gwen's eyes were wide with fear and worry for her husband who had run into the blazing house. She could see more flames now and began to feel the immense heat radiating from the blaze. Windows popped and shattered, spewing glass onto the lawn, releasing heavy smoke into the air. Gwen tried to get the old woman up from the ground. The poor woman could not break her gaze from the sight of her burning home. Gwen pulled the frail lady into her lap and held her like a child. In the chaos, a crowd had begun to gather. A young girl placed her hand lightly on Gwen's shoulder and asked if she could help. Gwen could not speak; she could only shake her head.

Before she could process the sounds, a fire truck with its sirens blaring, pulled up in front of the house. It effectively blocked Gwen's view of the family van. Even in all the mayhem, Gwen could still hear the singing voices of her daughters.

"Gwen, are you okay? Where is Ed?"

Gwen recognized Shawn's voice as he came out of the truck at a full run.

"He's in the house trying to help the old man, Shawn. You have to get him," Gwen sobbed as she replied.

Panic was starting to wash over her. She held the woman tighter as she watched on in horror. Where was her husband?

Without hesitation, Shawn threw on his respirator and headed to the front of the house. Other fireman were hooking up and rolling out hoses. Two others ran around to the back of the house and one or two were performing crowd control and trying to clear the area. An EMT strode up to Gwen and knelt down to check on the elderly woman. A news crew rolled up and a tall man jumped out snapping pictures. Flashes of light seemed to be everywhere. The chaos was unbelievable. Police cars were also on scene with their sirens and lights blaring.

The front yard was becoming overpowered by smoke and heat from the flames, making it dangerous for them to be there.

The EMT yelled to Gwen over the sirens and sounds of the flames and crowd, "Follow me, quickly."

Then, he reached beneath the woman and scooped her up, heading for the ambulance. Gwen followed on his heels, but turned to glance back at the blaze. She saw a figure emerge from behind the house. The smoke had taken over the area and Gwen squinted her eyes and raised her hand to shield her face from the heat of the inferno.

She was not sure who the man was until she heard the voice of her husband call out. He was covered in soot and coughing profusely, stumbling towards her. She stopped short and ran to him just as he went down on one knee. As she grabbed for Ed, a large window in the front of the house shattered and a fireman's axe protruded through the hole, raking glass away. Gwen looked up to see a leg appear, followed by the torso of Shawn.

"Get back," Shawn yelled as he ran towards his brother and sister-in-law, grabbing Ed under the arms and hustling them both away from the burning building.

Right on cue, the roof heaved over and caved to the ground spreading flames further out into the yard. The heat was intense as the onlookers' shocked cries were heard.

"I couldn't get to him. I tried, but his room was completely engulfed," Ed desperately said between coughing, wheezing breaths.

"I know you did all you could, buddy. Don't beat yourself up now," Shawn said to his brother as he helped him walk over to the back of an ambulance.

He eased his brother onto the rear of the ambulance, and then slipped an oxygen mask over his face.

"Try to relax and take deep breathes. We need to get those lungs cleared or you'll end up in the hospital. That was a crazy thing for you to do, Ed. Could you not try the 'hero' bit anymore? Try to remember who the firefighter in this family is from now on."

Shawn gave his brother a big grin and Ed relaxed a little as his wife put her arm around him. Shawn turned back to the scene of the fire. There was still a ton of work left to be done.

Gwen could hear the crying of the old woman from the back of another ambulance.

She knew someone must have told the woman her husband

was gone. Pain twisted Gwen's face, she felt terrible for the lady, but was relieved her own husband was safe and sound. Then it struck her…she could no longer hear her children singing.

She stopped for a moment and leaned her head to one side, trying to find the beautiful voices in all the madness around them. Nothing. Without a word, Gwen bolted for their van. Seeing his wife jump and run, Ed threw off the oxygen mask and ran after her, suddenly realizing why she was running.

Gwen approached the van, but saw the interior light was shining from within and the side door was open. How could her kids have opened that door? It did have child-safety latches. Didn't it? As she came around the back of the van with Ed on her heels, she could hear Aiden crying from inside. On the ground, spread out from the vehicle, were the remains of the pages her girls colored that evening in church and the copy of 'A Child's Hymnal' they always took with them. The recent newspaper headline, *Child Abducted from Local Area*, flashed through her mind. Gwen's world spun out of control. She screamed in terror.

****

I watched in silence and shadow: everyone trying so desperately to help the poor old couple. No one giving a second thought to those precious, little girls in the van. Oh, how sweetly they sang. I made my way towards them and no one even noticed me. They were almost as beautiful as the last one. I swore there would be no more. I just couldn't help myself...didn't want to help myself. As I slid the van door open, the two girls with the angelic voices stopped singing and smiled up at me with such trusting, loving faces. Pure love. I couldn't help but smile back. It was then, I knew they were mine.

EIGHT

Skip

Skyler Anthony Perryman could never be called average or ordinary...not by any stretch of the imagination. Skip was the kind of guy women loved and he kept a different one every day of the week, just to prove that point. An extremely good-looking man, he was six feet tall with dark, blond hair, blue eyes and that chiseled physique that screamed sexuality. More like a *Calvin Klein* model, he constantly kept stubble on his face, but it worked for him and added to his appeal. He dressed in the finest clothing, always in style, smoked the finest European cigarettes money could buy and had an annoying habit of flipping the top of his gold cigarette lighter when he talked. With a smile that would light a room, his voice was like fine cognac, smooth and warm and tantalizing to the ears. He was almost as handsome as he was rich. Even some men would question their sexuality when Skip was around. He was 'fathers-lock-up-your-daughters' good looking and he was well aware of it.

Skip Perryman lived a charmed life and was spoiled by his doting mother, Rochelle, who believed he could do no wrong. She lavished her son with money and expensive gifts...nothing was too good for her only child.

John Perryman, Skip's father, learned years earlier to go

along with Skip's musings or risk sparking the maternal fires of his wife. So, John remained always agreeable when dealing with him.

Since high school, women had always thrown themselves at Skip. His stature as rugby team captain and high standing in the community only added to his intrigue. His interests varied from expensive cars and gambling to collecting extravagant types of alcohol during his world travels.

He had 'side ventures' as he liked to call them, which consisted of dealing cocaine and methamphetamines to the rich, affluent patrons in his circle. He also had a darker, seedier side when it came to his personal preferences for sexual extremes that included bondage and his predatory infatuation with young, easily influenced girls. Occasionally, Skip would step too far out of line with his sexual exploits and Rochelle would be there to clean up the mess.

One of these occasions was while attending an ivy-league collage: a drunken Skip picked up a girl at a frat party and decided to take her back to his apartment. There, he plied her with alcohol and drugs and proceeded to practice his bondage and S&M sexual games on her not-so-willing personage. Ball-gagged and tied to a bed for fourteen hours, Skip repeatedly raped and sodomized the young girl, continually feeding her and himself, Absinthe and Ecstasy. As the drugs and alcohol finally overcame him, he passed out, leaving the girl to escape from her captor and run, naked and beaten to her parents.

They immediately contacted the police, who converged on his apartment with a vengeance. Skip awoke to the sight of police breaking in his door and surrounding him. He was roughly hauled away in hand cuffs, as the police scoured his apartment, taking pictures and collecting evidence.

Skip, being well known even in this college town, already gained a reputation with the police, who where confident they would be able to nail him for unlawful confinement, kidnapping and statutory rape and sodomy of a minor. It turned out the girl was only fifteen-years-old and her parents were prominent citizens who did not intend to back off.

When the Perryman's were contacted as to Skip's predicament, they came out with guns blazing. Hiring one of the top criminal lawyers in the country, they not only succeeded in getting him out of the charges, but also managed to have the record sealed even though he was well past the age of adulthood. Skip got off with a slap on the wrist and a few hours of community service. No one ever knew just how much Rochelle Perryman paid to hide his indiscretions, only that the price must have been astronomical.

Skip was dismissed from his school, but it wasn't long until he was again ensconced at another prominent school in another college town.

With the help of his mother's money, he finally managed to graduate from college with a degree in banking. He joined his father's investment firm and did rather well, all things considered.

Whenever John Perryman needed someone to make a trip to New York, Los Angeles or London, he would send Skip. His father knew he would do everything he could to increase the size of the family wealth, knowing full well that it would all be his some day. Mr. Perryman also thought these trips would keep Skip occupied somewhere other than Aberdeen and that maybe his extra-curricular activities might not spill over onto the local female population. John was also aware of Skip's drug business and thought if he was not available to his clientele maybe his business would dwindle off enough to discourage him from continuing to deal.

Skip knew what his father was doing and often thought how singularly naive he was. He not only kept up his drug sales to the locals—having long ago placed a police officer or two in his back pocket—but also managed to deal drugs to the people in his circles in the other cities he frequented.

He never really loved his father because he felt the man had never taken any time with him or been there when the need arose. It was always his mother who had been there for him and Skip felt slighted by his dad. He respected what his father accomplished in life and of course, loved the fact that because of his father's hard work, he would always have all the things in life he felt he deserved, but there really was no love between them. This fact tended to make Skip angry under the surface. He often commented he hated his father and couldn't see him in the ground soon enough, though most believed this was a comment made out of greed and the desire to control his father's money. Those close to him knew it stemmed from something much deeper.

On this particular day, Skip had not been in town long. He had just returned from a business trip to Los Angeles and was in town at the local liquor store, picking up a shipment of imported scotch he'd ordered a few weeks ago. As he glanced out the front window of the store, he saw the retreating figure of a beautiful woman and Skip being Skip, curiosity got the best of him.

"On second thought Mike, could you have this stuff delivered...I see someone I need to speak to," he said to the store owner while still staring at the woman across the street.

"Sure can. It will be there before noon," the store owner replied as Skip was stepping out the front door.

He headed in the direction of the woman who was now standing next to an older model car, about to get in and leave. Just then the woman turned slightly. Skip knew her instantly and walked up behind her.

"Hello, darlin'...miss me?" Skip purred right into Sloanne's ear.

Sloanne turned and drew back as she realized who had just spoken to her.

"Yes, Skip...but if you'll stand still while I back out, I'll try not to miss you again," Sloanne said in her sweetest, most sarcastic voice.

"Oh, come on, darlin', don't be that way. You know you still care about ol' Skip. We had some good times, didn't we?"

Skip's sticky-sweet voice gushed over Sloanne as he repeatedly flicked a gold lighter in his hand.

"Yes we did. You, more than me."

Sloanne was smiling, but the smile was full of disdain, as she intended it to be.

"Aw, don't be like that. We were just kids back then. We're grown up now. I've changed and I'm sure you have too. I'm working with my dad and doing quite well. I hear you're doing great too. You certainly are looking great. Same beauty you always were only now you have that 'big city class' about you. I like that. So sexy. I always knew you were meant for better than this town. And just look at you. The boys would be after you themselves if they could see you now."

Skip was still smooth as glass, but Sloanne was not at all impressed with him. Not like she had once been and it nearly turned her stomach to hear him talk.

"Skip, I wish I could stay and chat, but I have to get back to Chloe's. She not doing well and I need to be there."

"Oh yeah...your friend Chloe. Heard about her kid being missing. Cute kid that Danni. I've seen them a few times around town and even thought about asking Chloe out for dinner. But I'm not really into the 'ready-made family' thing. Too bad about the kid though," Skip didn't really care, but he wanted Sloanne and would say what was necessary to get her. "I was hoping you and I could get together before you leave town again. How about we have dinner tonight…just for old times sake?"

"I don't think that's really a good idea. Anyway, I need to stick close to Chloe until something turns up with Danni. She's really a wreck."

Sloanne didn't want to be having this conversation and the quicker she could get away from him, the better.

"You know, my parents are putting up a lot of money to help with the search for that kid. Least you could do is be nice and have a little dinner with me. I'd hate to tell my momma how disappointed I was that you snubbed me this way," Skip said a little viciously, still flipping the fancy lighter.

Sloanne felt trapped and knowing how much Skip's family would be able to aid in the monetary side of the search for Danni, she was afraid to turn him down, but was so repulsed at the same time. *Damn it*, how did she manage to get herself into this?

"Well Skip, since I'm obviously backed into a corner on this, I suppose I'll relent and let you have your way. I could meet you tonight at that new restaurant down the street, 'La Veranda', at about seven, can you do that?" Sloanne said in a not so friendly tone.

"Sure, darlin'. Sounds like a plan. Now you run along and do whatever it is you need to and I'll see you tonight. Wear something sexy for ol' Skip, okay?"

As he slithered away, Sloanne could not believe the disgusting, filthy way she felt after talking to him. She just wanted to run home and shower. And now she had to try to sit and endure a meal with the man. She had to get out of there, so she jumped into Chloe's car and headed for the house, wondering how she'd ever get through the evening ahead.

Skip turned to watch as Sloanne drove away, thinking about how he'd won the battle of wills with her. He slipped out one of his expensive cigarettes and placed it between his lips. As he stood there contemplating the evening ahead, he flicked the lighter in a smooth movement that lit the flame, then immediately extinguished it as the lid came back down. Over and over he flicked the lighter in that nervous way he had, all the while thinking about Sloanne and what he would like to do to her.

Finally, he lit his cigarette and then crossed the street to leave, smiling to himself at the evening's prospect.

NINE

Obstacles

As she drove away, Sloanne thought about how uncomfortable she felt around Skip and also about everything that happened years ago when they were an item and she became addicted.

She wondered how she was so naive and so easily misled. She once was in love with Skip and trusted him with her heart. He had been in love with her body and the fact that she was not so well-to-do. She guessed he loved her in his way, but the money and the drugs were his main concern and when push came to shove, he chose that life over her. She had been well into the drugs by the time Skip pushed her out and by then, her parents and Patty were onto what was going on. They immediately stepped in and rescued her from herself and she barely missed Skip during all the turmoil of rehab.

During rehab, she met Mr. Miera, CEO of The Miera Architectural Firm in New York. He and Sloanne hit it off immediately and he saw something in her that she, herself, did not see. He was a much older gentleman of Spanish descent, whose parents came to America to live the dream. They never had, but they made sure he'd been lucky enough to get a decent education which allowed him to build his business from the ground up. He looked the part of an early 40's-era screen lover: thin mustache, slicked-back, jet black hair and little piercing black eyes. He always carried a silver-handled cane, but it was only for show as he could get around better than most twenty year olds. Mr. Miera never told anyone his exact age, but to look at him and his accomplishments, most people assumed he was in his late sixties.

Never having married or fathered any children of his own, he took Sloanne under his wing and helped her realize her potential. Rumor around the office was that Mr. Miera would leave his firm and everything he had to Sloanne one day, but Sloanne dismissed this for what it was, office rumor. She hoped the wonderful man, who was her friend and business mentor, would live forever.

Sloanne's train of thought went back to Chloe and Danni and she was glad she could be here for them. But as time ticked away, she was becoming more and more fearful about what happened to Danni and how the investigation was progressing. Patty told Sloanne several times that the first forty-eight hours were the most crucial and when most missing kids were found. That time had come and gone and Sloanne was beginning to have doubts about whether Danni would be found unharmed. She didn't know how she would be able to continue to keep up a brave front for Chloe and she knew that Chloe would be able to see right through her cheerful façade. How would she ever look her friend in the eye and tell her things would be okay, when she was beginning to doubt it herself?

Sloanne maneuvered the Honda through the well-lit street and around the corner of the intersection, where just days before, she stood trying to help a dying man. Her mind wondered back to that scene and the events that took place there. She thought about the old couple's family and how they were doing.

Then she thought about Shawn Tyler. He was a surprise to her and she remembered how he was back in high school. Kind of *geeky,* was the only thing she could come up with as a description of the boy. But to look at him now was a completely different thing. She remembered his blue-gray eyes looking into hers and the quirky half-smile he'd given her. She smiled to herself, but then frowned as she thought she must be evil for even thinking good thoughts about a man, when all this sadness was surrounding her.

As Sloanne drove down Chloe's street, she thought about how different it looked now, as compared to how chaotic it was the night she arrived. There were no police cars or news crews or hordes of searchers on Chloe's front law. It was just a pretty, little street in a nice neighborhood, in a quiet town except there were no children out playing. The neighborhood parents were being more cautious about their kids and the street appeared more like a ghost town.

The police were still monitoring Chloe's phone calls and coming by at regular intervals, but their presence was no longer constant. The searchers had thinned and although they were still looking for Danni, they were no longer based in the front yard. The search parties now consisted less of law enforcement and more of neighbors and a few friends. People were beginning to lose hope that Danni would be found and it made Sloanne very sad. She knew how hopeless it was beginning to be and she felt terrible for Chloe.

Sloanne pulled up in the drive and got out of the car, hating to go in the house, but knowing she had to. She mentally forced herself to adjust her somber attitude and opened the front door of Chloe's home.

Chloe was sitting on the sofa in front of the TV with the sound turned down. She immediately got up and went to Sloanne as she came in the door. Sloanne knew that Chloe was still trying to have a positive attitude, but the anxious look on her face told the tale.

"Have you heard anything from Patty?" Sloanne asked Chloe, taking her hand.

"He called a few minutes ago and he's on his way over. He sounded a bit rattled, but said he'd explain when he got here. What do you think is happening, Sloanne?" Chloe was visibly shaken.

"I don't know Chloe, but this could be a good thing. Maybe the police have a lead or have found a clue as to Danni's whereabouts. Don't think the worst until we hear what Patty has to say," Sloanne felt afraid, but didn't want Chloe to know. She thought maybe a change of subject would distract her 'til Patty arrived.

"You'll never guess who accosted me on the street in town,"

Sloanne said, rolling her eyes.

"Uh Oh...not Skip? He doesn't waste any time does he? What did the scumbag have to say?" Chloe said, obviously trying to distract her own thoughts.

"Well, he had the nerve to ask if I'd missed him and sort of demanded that I have dinner with him. Ah shit! I can't believe I'm going to do this," Sloanne said with a huff.

"I can't believe you're going to do it either, Sloanne. Have you lost your mind? Why in the world would you consider going anywhere with that man?" Chloe said as her concern shifted to Sloanne.

"It was kind of an either/or situation and I, of course, got shoved into a corner. I guess the only thing to do is to just get it over and done with as quickly as possible. I mean, really...how bad can it be? I did once love the guy and it is only dinner," Sloanne said trying to make herself feel better about the situation.

"Okay. Well, it probably would not be a good idea to let Patty find out about this. I believe the term, 'blow-a-gasket' would be putting it mildly," Chloe returned. "You better make sure you have this dinner in a very public place and you should be careful, Sloanne. Skip is a real creep and some people say he's a little on the pervy side. He's not the same guy you dated in high school and you should keep that in mind."

"We're meeting at 'La Veranda' at 7 p.m. Since I've never

been there, I don't know how public it is," Sloanne replied to Chloe. "What do you think?"

"Pretty high class place, but it should be public enough. You should try to keep it short and call me the minute you leave there, please. I don't want to have to worry about you too."

Chloe bit off her words just as a short knock at the door sounded and in strode Patty. He kissed Sloanne and Chloe. Sloanne could see there was something troubling him. She was almost afraid to hear what he had to say.

"Have you girls been watching the news? There have been some new developments. I don't want you two to get freaked out, but the Aberdeen police think we may have a serial kidnapper on our hands. Two more kids were taken last night from the scene of a fire. The parents had gotten out to help, leaving the kids in the back seat, right in plain sight. Next thing you know, they were gone without a trace. Everything has gone national now. The Maryland State Police are really getting involved and Danni's picture, along with pictures of the two other kids, are being circulated all along the upper East Coast. This is bad, but good from our point of view, because now Danni is getting more coverage." Patty tried to sound hopeful. "Turn up the sound and switch the channel to CNN. Let's see what's being broadcast."

Chloe, face drained of color, sank down to the sofa while Sloanne stepped over to retrieve the remote, switching the channel and turning up the sound as she sat down next to her. The news caster was going over the details of both cases.

"Police in Aberdeen Maryland are tracking leads today, on what appears to be, a serial kidnapper on the loose. In the time span of just over a week, three children, all females ranging in age from nine to thirteen years, have been abducted from accident scenes while their parents were attempting to lend a helping hand. Maryland State Police officials are assuming command of the investigation and have given this statement to the media: 'We want the public to be aware of the situation and cautious at all times. We are working tirelessly to identify the perpetrator of these heinous crimes and return these children safely home. Anyone with any information should contact the Maryland State Police at 410-386-3101 or the National Center for Missing and Exploited Children at 1-800-THELOST (1-800-843-5678)'."

The newscaster went on: "Thirteen-year-old Danielle Jacobs, seen here, was taken from a grocery store in downtown Aberdeen, during which time, her mother was attempting to revive a heart attack victim. Just last night, twin nine-year-olds, Kimmi and Kammi Tyler, were taken from the scene of a house fire as their parents were trying to rescue an occupant of the home. There are few leads in either case and the Aberdeen Police are keeping a tight lip on the investigation. We will continue to update you with photos and breaking news throughout the remainder of this tragically, developing news story. This is Kelsey Collins reporting," and the scene quickly switched back to the news desk.

"Oh my god…what does this mean?"

Chloe stood up and stammered, more to herself than to Sloanne and Patty. Her face took on that look of complete and utter pain that Sloanne had come to dread seeing.

"Now, Chloe, you have be strong and have hope for Danni. The police are working as hard as they can to find her and people are still searching for her. We have to concentrate on that and continue to pray that Danni will be found soon. If this is a serial kidnapper, he may make a mistake that will lead the police right to him and to Danni. We have to keep believing that she is all right and that she'll be home soon. I know you are scared and worried, but you have to stay strong…we both do. Patty is helping the police as much as he can and I have faith that he knows what needs to be done," Sloanne said.

"I actually think the two girls who were taken last night, are the kids of Ed and Gwen Tyler. I think Ed's brother Shawn, went to school with you guys. Do either of you remember him? He is a fireman in town and his firehouse crew is helping with the search parties," Patty interjected.

"Wait a minute…Shawn Tyler…the fireman…you've got to be kidding me. I just talked to him a few days ago at that big accident on Main St. Remember I told you about it, Chloe?" Sloanne said speaking to Patty and Chloe at the same time.

"Accident on Main St.? You mean the elderly couple who died in that big wreck? Wait a minute…what the hell were you doing there?" Patty asked incredulously.

"Uh…I meant to tell you about that, Patty. I was at the grocery store and it all happened so fast. I was standing by the car one minute and standing in the wreckage the next. It was almost like I was watching Mom and Dad and I guess my emotions just took over and well, Shawn sort of plucked me right out of the center of the fray and that was about it." Sloanne stammered.

"Sloanne, have you lost your mind? What were you thinking? I heard there was fuel everywhere and even the rescue crew couldn't get in there 'til the power was shut off. I can't believe you walked out into the middle of that hell. Sloanne, you are the only thing I have in this world and I'd appreciate it if you would try to be a little more careful in the future. You could have been killed."

Patty was livid and it made Sloanne feel like a child. She had been stupid and was just now realizing what a dumb thing she had done. Patty's face was twisted with fear and anger, but then it took on the pitiful sad look of a man who had lost most of the people he'd loved in life. Patty reached out and grabbed Sloanne and dragged her into his arms and then as a second thought, he grabbed Chloe too and gathered them both into a big emotional embrace.

"I'm sorry, Patty. I don't know what came over me. All I

could see was Mom and Dad and I just felt compelled to help those old people," Sloanne mumbled into Patty's chest.

"Shhh, now. Let's don't talk about this anymore. You're safe and that's what matters," Patty almost sobbed.

After a moment, he stepped back and straightened himself, trying not to let them see how emotional he had gotten.

"I think you two should get out of the house for a bit. Why don't we drive over to the Tyler's home and see how they are making out. I need to talk to Detective Howard and I'm sure he's there now. You girls get ready and we'll head over." Patty said with concern.

By this time, Chloe had again sat down on the sofa and was watching the news reports.

There was a tap at the front door and Patty stepped over to see who it was. Two of Chloe's neighbors came in. It was the same two ladies that Sloanne had seen there the night she arrived. The ladies came in and greeted everyone and then made their way over to Chloe.

"How are you, dear?" one of the ladies asked as they both sat and in turn hugged Chloe. The three of them began to talk quietly together on the sofa.

"We were just on our way out to check on the Tyler family," Sloanne interjected.

"No, I'm not leaving," Chloe said forcefully. "I think I

should stay here in case Danni comes home. What if she escapes and comes home and I'm not here? What would she think? No, I need to be here, but you and Patty should go. I'm sure the Tyler's are in bad shape and you two can help. I'll be okay here with Mrs. Cooper and her daughter. Please, go and help, Patty. Help the police find this mad man." Chloe said in a quiet voice.

"Are you sure, Chloe? I don't feel right leaving you here alone. I can stay." Sloanne said.

"No, no really. I'm not alone and I need you to be out there helping Patty and the police. Please go. Just let me know what's going on." Chloe replied.

"Chloe…are you sure. I think it would be good for you to get out of this house," Patty added.

"Patty, I know you mean well, but I'm sure…go!"

"Okay then. We won't be gone long and I'll call if we hear anything new."

Sloanne knew that Chloe's mind was made up and she felt that her time would be better spent helping in the investigation. Since Chloe had someone to stay with her, Sloanne gathered her things and left with Patty.

As they rode through town, there was a somber quiet in the car. Sloanne was thinking ahead to the Tyler's. She considered all that had taken place and her mind was going through all the information they had so far.

100

"You know Sloanne, I love having you back here in Aberdeen, but I really wanted you back here because I think you have a mind for this kind of investigation. You've always been an analytical thinker and that's just what we need here to help solve this case. You always were a chip off the ol' block when it came to police work and your dad and I always hoped you would follow in our footsteps. You see things differently than most people, more like a cop than most cops I know," Patty was thinking out load now and she smiled.

"Patty, if things hadn't turned out like they did, I probably would have gone to the academy. You know, I'd thought about being a cop more than once, but my life took a strange turn and it just didn't seem to be in the cards."

"You would have made an excellent law enforcement officer, Sloanne and you still could. Have you thought about it lately?"

Patty seemed to be fishing now and Sloanne knew what he wanted to hear. Patty and her father had been proud to be in law enforcement and nothing could have meant more to them both, than for her to become a cop. She had always known this, but nothing in her life had gone as planned and she settled into her job in New York and was as content as she thought possible. She had not given police work much thought in the last few years, but now she was aware of a feeling of needing to help others and to immerse herself in the law enforcement world. It made her feel closer to her father and to Patty and it just felt right.

"I really haven't thought about it in years until now, but I'm not sure I'm cut out for this kind of work. I'm afraid I'd get too close to the victims and that would cloud my judgment. I'd be more of a hindrance than a help and that would not be good. Objectivity is not one of my stronger suits, so I just don't know," Sloanne mused to Patty.

"Well, kiddo, sounds like you're still not giving yourself enough credit. You have a good heart and good instincts. I'd back you on whatever you decided, you know. I don't know a cop on the force who wouldn't consider it an honor to work with you," Patty said while grinning a sly smile.

Just then, they pulled up to the curb and Patty put the car in park.

"Looks like we'll have to walk from here," Patty said. Sloanne looked out the window and the scene was a replay of the night she arrived.

Police cars were scattered up the street, people were milling around getting ready to form search parties and of course, there was the ever-present media van. Sloanne could see the balding head of Birney Sullivan in the crowd.

"Damn, that Birney Sullivan sure gets around. What a piece of work he is," Sloanne hissed.

"He's just doing his job, kiddo and some of his photos have

actually netted the police some good leads on past cases. Give him a break, okay?" Patty replied. Sloanne sighed and thought maybe Patty was right, but Birney still gave her the creeps and she just didn't like the guy.

She and Patty got out of the car and proceeded up to the front door of the Tyler home. Sloanne knew that the Tylers would be in bad shape and she was not looking forward to the sadness she was about to encounter, but she felt that she might be able to help them in some way. She was also interested in finding out all she could about how the two small girls were taken. As she ran her fingers through her hair in that nervous way she had, she realized she felt a strong urge to be there for Shawn too and wondered why she felt so close to him. Maybe it was just the kinship of having people they both cared for disappear in a similar manner, but Sloanne wanted to help him and his family all she could.

Patty knocked at the door and it was opened by Detective Howard. Sloanne recognized him as the man who had spoken for the police the night she arrived at Chloe's and figured he had to be the chief detective of Aberdeen's force. She and Patty stepped into the foyer and stopped there to have a word with the detective. Patty asked him if there was anything new with the investigation and they talked momentarily about the details of the case. Then, Detective Howard turned to Sloanne.

"I knew your father, Sloanne. He was a good cop and a good

man. We were all sad when he and your mother died. I always thought that maybe you'd become a cop one day. You know, take after your old man. Your dad thought you had the instincts for this work and he said many times he believed you were tough enough. I'm glad we have Patty helping us with this case. An extra pair of eyes and point of view is what we need."

Sloanne smiled at the Detective. It was surprising to hear from someone other than Patty, that her father felt this way about her. Sloanne and her parents had hardly ever spoken of her future when she was a kid and to know her dad thought she would make a good cop, that he thought she was a strong person, made her feel a sense of pride she had not felt in quite a while. It also made her smile to think of her father and how much he and her mother loved her.

As they walked into the living room of the Tyler's home, Sloanne immediately heard the sound of gentle crying. It was a heart-wrenching sound and Sloanne simply walked over and placed her hand on Gwen Tyler's shoulder.

Gwen looked up at Sloanne with such a deep sadness that Sloanne nearly gasped, but she tried to control her feelings as she walked around the chair Gwen was sitting in and knelt down in front of her. Sloanne took Gwen's hands in her own and simply looked up into her face. Sloanne had never met Gwen Tyler before, but what passed between them was comforting to Gwen and she seemed to take strength from Sloanne's grasp.

Patty again spoke briefly with Detective Howard and then Ed Tyler stood and shook Patty's hand, but it was a listless gesture and he immediately sat back down. The detective introduced Patty to the Tylers and told them how he was helping with the investigation. He then introduced Sloanne and told them she was the best friend of Chloe Jacobs, the woman whose daughter had been previously taken.

"We were so sorry to hear about your friend's daughter. We read about her being abducted in the paper, but we just didn't realize the danger until our babies were taken. It was stupid of me to leave my children alone, but I never thought anything like this could ever happen to them. I've never really thought something like this could happen in our town and especially not to our kids. You must think we are terrible parents for leaving the kids in the van alone, but I swear we never even considered something could happen to them," Gwen seemed to be begging Sloanne to understand what happened and Sloanne immediately stopped her.

"Gwen, please don't think that way. My friend Chloe was trying to save a man's life and someone took her daughter right out from under her. She never thought this could happen either. I don't think it does any good for you all to beat yourselves up for trying to be a Good Samaritan and help someone. It's the person who took these kids who is to blame. Not you and not Chloe. Do you understand?" Sloanne said with conviction. Gwen Tyler shook her head, but Sloanne could see in her eyes that she blamed herself and

Sloanne felt her pain.

"Ed, would you mind telling us exactly what took place last night leading up to the children being taken?" Patty asked, his professional, police voice in full force now.

"If you aren't comfortable discussing this in front of civilians, please let me know and we'll do this later," Detective Howard interjected.

"I'll be happy to go outside if it will help, Ed," Sloanne said as she stood to leave. Sloanne wanted to hear the story, but understood the implications.

Ed reached up and grabbed Sloanne's hand to stop her and replied, "No, you should hear this."

He started to relay the tale of the fire and the events leading up to the abduction of his twin daughters. Sloanne could see the agony on his face and the utter pain and loss in the room was thick enough to cut with a knife. She felt so sorry for these nice people and for the little girls who were missing. Tears began to rim her eyes as she reached over and gently touched Gwen's hand again.

Sloanne listened to the story through to the end, quietly thinking to herself. She could almost see the scene in her head and wondered about the similarities between this case and Danni's abduction. The fact that both abductions took place while the children's parents were trying to help in emergency situations, made Sloanne wonder how the abductor planned and made himself available at both scenes. Was it a coincidence or was there something else going on here? How could the abductor know these things would happen in advance and how could he or she have been so conveniently present for both?

Sloanne made a mental note of questions she wanted to ask Patty as Ed Tyler finished telling the sad tale. She felt horrified someone would take innocent children, but she also felt strangely invigorated by the events and knew she wanted to help in any way she could.

Gwen Tyler was sitting stone-faced and Sloanne asked her if there was anything she could help her with. Gwen asked if Sloanne would help her upstairs to her bed and Sloanne walked with her up the stairs, still holding her hand and gently telling her not to worry, that everything was being done that could be done. She hoped what she was telling Gwen was a comfort, but she knew Gwen Tyler was feeling her world crashing around her, just as Chloe was. She knew no matter what she said, this woman had lost her children and no amount of soothing would heal that pain. Gwen Tyler and Chloe Jacobs were two women with one thing in common—the loss of their children. Sloanne had some idea of how bad they were hurting, but she also knew only a mother could understand this kind of pain.

Sloanne helped Gwen settle into her bed and covered her with a throw. She then went back downstairs as Patty, Ed Tyler and Detective Howard were finishing their conversation. Sloanne suddenly thought of Shawn.

"Ed, where is Shawn? I wanted to talk with him for a moment and we thought he would be here with you," Sloanne asked.

"It's Shawn's forty-eight hour shift at the firehouse. He just felt so useless around here that he figured work was the best place to be. He's really torn up about the girls, being so close to them and all. I don't think he knows how to handle all this sadness. He's always been a sensitive guy and this is almost too much for him, Sloanne. I know you two went to school together and he mentioned seeing you the other day, before all this happened. He smiled when he told us about seeing you at that accident and he seemed excited about meeting you again. He doesn't get that way about many people. You think maybe you could go by the firehouse and see him? I know it would help him, if you could," Ed said in a quiet tone.

It was obvious to Sloanne that Ed was concerned about his younger brother and Sloanne could tell they were close.

"Of course I will, Ed. I don't know how much help I can be, but I'll certainly give it my best shot. Don't worry," Sloanne replied to the big, sad man standing in front of her.

They said their goodbyes to Ed and Detective Howard and Sloanne told Ed to tell his wife that she would be back soon to talk with her more. Patty placed his hand on Sloanne's back and steered her out the door, down the steps and back in the direction of his car. They both got in and sat quietly as Patty headed the car towards the main firehouse in Aberdeen.

The firehouse was situated off Main St. about two miles from the biggest intersection in Aberdeen. The same intersection where Sloanne had run into Shawn only a week or so ago. The firehouse was set back from Main St. about one hundred feet and the drive up to the main entrance was wide enough for two large fire trucks to exit at the same time. On one side of the drive was a cut-off that led into a small parking area for the firemen who worked this station. On the other side of the wide drive was another cut-off that led around to the back of the station and Sloanne could see the firehouse had two large bays and were open at both ends with large roll-up doors. There was also a windowed, single door next to one of the bay doors. Sloanne could see, the door led into a dispatch office.

Sloanne knew the shifts here were, two-days-on and three-days-off. A crew of six firemen and three rescue EMTs were at the station at all times and the men worked, ate and slept here during their respective shifts. Sloanne could see that there were two, large, fire trucks in the front bays of the firehouse. One truck was a pumper full of hoses and the other was a ladder truck with a large, extension ladder and a big, steering wheel on the back. Behind one of the fire trucks, she could see a rescue vehicle backed into the bay facing away from the front and she could tell the truck exited by way of the drive that circles to the back of the firehouse.

Patty turned into the wide drive and then cut into the parking area, pulling into a parking spot. Sloanne hoped they wouldn't be intruding on the day-to-day work being carried out at the firehouse, but she was anxious to speak to Shawn, so she got out of the car and headed, with Patty, up the walk to the dispatch office door. Patty pulled open the door and held it for Sloanne. She walked in and up to the desk. Behind the desk sat a friendly looking man in a fireman's uniform and he smiled and asked her if he could help. She noticed there was a name tag sewn to the man's pocket stating his name was, 'Johnston'.

"Yes, sir. Would it be possible for us to have a word with Shawn Tyler?" Sloanne shyly asked the smiling man.

"Sure, he's around back rolling some hoses. You can just step out this side door and go straight out the back. You'll see him out there," the fireman said continuing to smile at Sloanne.

"Thank you so much. We won't be in the way, will we?" Sloanne said back to the man and he just smiled and shook his head.

She thanked him and she and Patty proceeded out the door and towards the back of the station house. As they stepped through the big, bay door, she saw Shawn standing at a distance, with his back to them, rolling a large hose. As he pulled up the hose, she noticed his broad back and the way the muscles bunched and relaxed with the motion he was making. Another fireman was standing a few feet away from Shawn, facing towards the firehouse feeding the hose to him and the man made a motion that caused Shawn to turn around and look. As he saw Sloanne, his mouth formed into that quirky half-smile he had and he threw a hand up in a wave. Sloanne and Patty stopped where they were and waited while he finished rolling the hose he'd been working on. When he finished, he said something to the man who had been feeding him the hose and then turned and headed towards Sloanne and Patty.

As Shawn approached, his hand went up to his hair and he ran his fingers through it in a motion that reminded Sloanne of how, she herself would do, in nervous moments. It seemed odd to her that he had this same habit and she smiled at the weird coincidence. As Shawn drew closer, she could see his face looked more tired and drawn than she remembered from the day of the accident and she felt sorry that he and his family were going through this awful experience.

"Hey, Sloanne. I wasn't expecting to see you here. How is Chloe holding up?" he asked a bit breathless, but still smiling.

"She is doing as well as can be expected, Shawn. How are you?" she asked as she looked into his eyes.

She could immediately see the smile fade and sadness start to creep into his blue-gray eyes.

"I guess I'm doing okay too. It's Ed and Gwen I'm worried about. Those girls mean the world to them and they are devastated by all this. I just don't know what to do for them at this point. I feel kind of useless," Shawn replied averting his eyes towards the ground.

Sloanne knew he didn't want them to see how torn up he was over the situation.

"Let me introduce my godfather. This is Patrick Louchlin. He's my family," Sloanne smiled as she made the introductions and she saw Patty smile at her reference.

They shook hands and she could tell the two men immediately liked each other as they both smiled warmly.

"We've just come from your brother's house. We talked with Ed and Gwen and Ed told us about what happened last night. I'm so sorry this terrible thing has spilled over into your family, Shawn. Patty is helping the police with the investigation and I'm trying to do my part as well. Is there anything I can do for you? I hoped you would be with your family, but Ed said you felt like you needed to be at work," she said softly.

"I just couldn't stand watching my brother and sister-in-law agonize over this thing anymore and I figured since there was no way to help, I'd be better off here. At least I know I can be productive here instead of waiting around my place or Ed's feeling helpless." Shawn said sadly.

Sloanne's heart went out to the man and she could see how much he loved his family and how helpless he actually felt.

"Shawn, the police are doing everything they can and I know your nieces and Danni will be back home soon. We have to keep the faith and keep doing all we can to make that happen. I have to be strong for Chloe and you have to do the same for Ed and Gwen. We can never give up," she said trying to show him a brave front.

"Well, kiddo, I have to get back to the shop. Detective Howard will be coming by there in a bit and I don't want to miss him. I hate to rush you away, but it's getting late," Patty said. Turning to Shawn he continued, "It was really nice meeting you, Shawn. Next time, I hope it's under better circumstances," Patty again offered his hand to Shawn, who shook it and then turned to Sloanne.

"My shift ends here in thirty minutes, Sloanne. Do you think you could stick around 'til then? We could go have a coffee and I'll be glad to drop you at Chloe's. I don't think I am ready to face Ed and Gwen just yet. Do you have time?" Shawn asked hopefully.

Sloanne could see the sadness in his face, so she told him she would stay, walk Patty to his car and then wait for him out front.

Sloanne and Patty walked slowly back through the firehouse and out to Patty's car. Patty told Sloanne he would see her in the morning and kissed her cheek. Getting into his car, he gave her a smile as he backed out of the lot and left.

As Sloanne turned back to the firehouse she thought of all that happened in the short span of time she had been back in town. The sadness and hurt washed over her for her friend and for Shawn and his family. She felt resigned to do whatever she could to help all these people and their children to be reunited. She thought again about the children and what they must be going through. She also wondered if they would ever be seen alive again. She knew she should not even consider the possibility, but time was ticking away and she was feeling a strange premonition and was becoming more and more fearful that something bad was about to happen.

TEN

La Veranda

Sloanne walked back towards the firehouse. She knew she had thirty minutes to wait for Shawn so she took a seat on the bench sitting next to the door of the dispatch office. It was fairly comfortable and the weather was cool making it quite nice sitting there.

She was thinking about Shawn and his family. They seemed very close knit and it made her smile. She had no brothers or sisters and her parents were gone. Patty was the only family she had and he was not related to her. Chloe and Danni were like family too, but she knew it wasn't the same as having brothers and sisters of your own. She had always been jealous of people with big, happy families that were close and loving. She knew her parents loved her, but they were gone way too soon and she was rather lonely now.

She thought about Shawn and the kind of man he seemed to be. Obviously, he was close to his brother and his family, but Chloe told her Shawn's parents were gone too and she wondered if—even with his close brotherly ties—he was lonely like she was. He lived in Aberdeen all his life and since his family was here, he may not miss that family closeness the way she did. But she, living in New York, didn't see Patty, Chloe and Danni very often and it seemed as if her work had become her life. She wanted to do something about that, but so far she really had no reason to change anything. She never dated anyone, she only had a few friends in the city and they were people she worked with. She was in a rut as far as her personal life was concerned and she wished she could change that.

She thought Shawn was kind and very polite. His brother spoke about him as being sensitive. Now that was something you didn't run into very often—a sensitive man. He seemed different from the men she knew. When he spoke, he thought about what he would say before he said it and everything he did say was to the point, very precise and intelligent. She liked that about him. He was attractive for sure. She liked what she knew about Shawn Tyler so far and she wanted to know more.

"Hello." Shawn said simply and Sloanne looked up into his beautiful eyes and quirky grin.

"Hi."

She totally lost her train of thought in that one moment and now she could only smile back at him.

"Are you ready to go or should I sit down by you while you think about it a little longer?" he asked. "You were totally lost in your thoughts. Can I ask what you were thinking so hard about?"

"You can certainly ask, but I'd never be able to tell you…too much jumble in there." Sloanne said shyly, pointing to her head.

It was as if he had seen what she was thinking about and she was a little embarrassed at the idea of being caught.

"If you're ready for coffee, we can walk right down the street a couple blocks to the diner. You don't mind walking, do you?" Shawn teased her.

"Not at all. It's a really nice day and walking is always good," she said lightly.

They headed down the street in silence, but she felt comfortable and didn't feel like she had to say anything. It was nice to be this comfortable around someone. She glanced at Shawn a few times and noticed a slight smile on his face. Her curiosity made her wonder what he found amusing. She didn't want to be nosey, so she let it pass and they walked on until they reached the diner. He held the door for her and they took a booth at the far end of the long counter. The waitress came and Shawn ordered their coffee and she went away.

"I was wondering," Sloanne started and Shawn finished, "What I was smiling about a few minutes ago, right?"

"Well, yes, but how did you know that was what I was going to ask?"

"This may sound kind of strange to you, but I feel very comfortable around you. Even though we have only met twice since high school, both times I have instantly been at ease with you. Is that weird?"

He looked rather like he was happy, but also like he was afraid she actually would think it was weird.

"I think you must have been reading my mind back there because I was thinking the exact same thing," she smiled from under her lashes and he grinned back at her.

Then his face took on a more serious look and he hesitated.

"What do you think is going to happen to Danni and Kimmi and Kammi? I mean *really*, what do you think?" he asked, but she did not think she could tell him what she actually thought.

All she could do was look at him, as he looked back into her eyes. He thought he read something there that made his face drop into his hands before they went into his hair.

"God, Sloanne, if something happens to those kids, it would kill their parents. I don't know what I'd do if that happened. Those kids mean the world to Gwen and Ed would just be lost. I know Chloe would be just as devastated as Gwen and I know it would hurt you deeply as well. Is there anything else we can do to help with the investigation? Anything at all?" he agonized.

"Shawn, I don't know what is going to happen, but I know that there are very few clues; the small, blue or black sports car that was seen could have belonged to anyone. Danni's watch was found on the ground, so the police think there was a struggle of sorts, but they don't know how someone could have gotten Danni in their car…unless they drugged her," Sloanne said almost in a whisper. "They found absolutely no clues at all last night, so there is next to nothing to go on and it's been more than a week since Danni was taken. I'm finding it harder and harder to have faith that she will be found at all, but I'm still trying my best to appear hopeful for Chloe. It nearly kills me to look into her eyes now. I know she feels it too. I feel pretty hopeless."

Shawn watched Sloanne's demeanor change in a matter of seconds, but all he could do was reach over and lay his hand on hers as it rested on the table between them.

"Sloanne, I'll do whatever I can to help you, I swear. I don't want you to be alone now. This person, whoever is stealing these children, seems off the deep end and dangerous. What's to say, they might not try to kidnap someone older, a grown woman, like you or Chloe?"

Sloanne saw concern on his face and thought about what he was saying. She had not considered that possibility, but she felt, from what she knew of police work, that criminals, especially kidnappers or serial killers, usually stuck to an MO once it was established, but there was always that slim possibility. The thought made a chill run up her spine and she shivered slightly. Shawn immediately picked up on what she was feeling.

"I'm sorry if I scared you, Sloanne, but I want you to be scared enough to be careful. I really don't want anything to happen to you. I mean, I *really* don't want you to be hurt," Shawn said squeezing her hand slightly.

She looked into his eyes and could see concern there. She

knew it was for his family and for Chloe, but she also knew he was concerned for her as well. The look on his face gave her a warm feeling in her stomach that she had not felt in years. She smiled at him and he smiled back at her as they drank their coffee in silence.

****

Sloanne was running late for dinner with Skip and she was feeling dread thick and heavy in the car as she drove to the restaurant. She had quickly changed into a simple black dress and heels. She didn't want to give Skip the wrong impression, but the dresses she brought with her were plain and simple except for this one, which she packed on a whim. This dress was a little too low cut and a little too revealing, but it was the best she had. She was thinking she wanted to get this dinner over with as soon as possible without pissing Skip off and loosing the much needed financial backing from the Perrymans. She knew their money was funding some of the search parties and paying for printed flyers for distribution and she certainly didn't want those things to stop. She felt as if she was, once again, shoved into a corner where Skip was concerned and she didn't like it.

She pulled up in front of 'La Veranda', but then opted to park herself rather than use the valet. She wheeled to the side of the building and into a parking space. She was a little nervous, but calmed herself and strode confidently up to the front door of the restaurant. The doorman ushered her into the foyer. The host was a

120

handsome man in his late fifties and he quickly looked up from his reservation book and smiled at Sloanne.

"Good evening ma'am, Welcome to 'La Veranda'. Do you have a reservation?"

"Yes, Perryman?" Sloanne replied to the host with a smile.

"Ah, yes, Perryman, Table for two, right this way please. Your party is waiting for you," the host said with a gesture of his hand.

Sloanne followed the man through the restaurant to a more secluded area in the back. As they came around an ornate screen, Sloanne saw Skip sitting at a table with none other than John and Rochelle Perryman. She slowed and nearly turned to flee, but then remembered why she was here and continued to the table behind the host.

As they approached, Skip saw her and rose from his chair with a smile. As he did so, John Perryman looked around and seeing Sloanne, followed his son's lead. Rochelle Perryman turned to see who Skip's date was and when she spied Sloanne, a look of disdain crossed her face followed by a more pleasant expression that Sloanne knew was fake.

"Evening, darlin'," Skip uttered as he made a move to kiss Sloanne's cheek.

She nearly pulled back from his approach, but thought better of it and let him kiss her.

John then offered his hand to Sloanne with something of a smile and said, "How have you been, Sloanne? You look lovely, my dear."

Sloanne knew John Perryman didn't dislike her when she and Skip dated and even though his greeting was polite, she knew he could not be too kind while Rochelle was present.

"Thank you, John. I have been doing well. How have you been?" she answered him in a kind manner.

The host proceeded to seat Sloanne and take her drink order. Rochelle began to speak to Sloanne in that haughty manner she had.

"Sloanne, we had no idea it was you Skip was seeing tonight. Now I understand why he was hesitant to tell us whom he was having dinner with. You certainly have changed from that scruffy, little Irish girl he dated in high school. So much more poised and elegant."

Rochelle had all ten claws out tonight.

"Why thank you, Rochelle. I must say you have not changed a bit. If I didn't know you better, I'd almost have taken that as a compliment," Sloanne replied to the woman.

She always felt inferior to Rochelle and her comment did little to change that as Sloanne was sure it was meant to.

"Ladies, let's play nicely," Skip cooed. "We've all changed, haven't we?"

"We were just finishing dinner when we saw Skip come in

and thought we would stop by his table before leaving," John said, obviously trying to mask the sarcasm that oozed from Rochelle.

She shot her husband a baleful glance and then it was gone just as quickly. Everyone was seated   and a short moment passed before anyone spoke.

"Sloanne, we're so sorry about your friend's daughter. Have there been any leads in the case?" John asked more to mask the silence than for information.

"No, John. No other leads have been forthcoming. I suppose you heard two more children were taken last night?" Sloanne replied.

"Horrible thing. Imagine a mother leaving her children alone while she tries to help a complete stranger," Rochelle spat out. "This family will do whatever is necessary to help in the investigation. We can't have things like this going on in our community. Why, it makes the price of real estate just plummet."

Sloanne could hardly believe even Rochelle—bitch that she was—would say such a horrible thing. She was aware that her mouth was open and she consciously closed it. She was livid, but she knew she needed to be calm.

"Rochelle, I hardly think that Gwen and Ed Tyler would think what they did was wrong. They love their children dearly, but there was an emergency situation. A man was burning to death in his bed. What would you have done?" Sloanne asked in a controlled voice.

"On that thought, I think it's time you two said goodnight, Mother, John," Skip smoothly slid into the conversation as he stood up and waved his hand in a manner that dismissed his mother and father.

"I think you are absolutely right, Skip. Rochelle, shall we go?" John asked.

Rochelle's face was priceless at this point. She obviously wanted to say something more to Sloanne on this subject, but the wave of Skip's hand sealed her fate and she resignedly stood up from the table and gathered her purse.

Then, her face changed to one of utter sweetness as she said, "So good to see you again, Sloanne. Tell Chloe we'll keep her in our prayers."

At that, Rochelle kissed her son's cheek and turned to walk away.

"Nice seeing you again, Sloanne," John Perryman said with a slight bow and he turned and followed his wife.

"Sorry, darlin', you know how Mom is about her baby boy?" Skip said with a sneer.

Sloanne was grateful to Skip for dismissing his mother in such a manner, but now she felt anxious at the thought of being left alone with him.

The waiter appeared and Skip ordered for them both. He then began to talk about what he had been doing for the last twelve years.

He talked about working with his dad and the trips he made for the company. He talked about his possessions and the wealth he accumulated over the years. But mostly, he talked about his conquests. All the while he talked, Sloanne watched him chain smoke an expensive brand of European cigarettes. But what she noticed most was the fact that before he would light one, he would flick the lighter open and then closed one time before he lit his cigarette. She thought it was a strange habit, but many people did many things when they talked and she dismissed it as a tick.

Their dinner was brought to the table and served while Skip continued to talk. He would occasionally ask Sloanne a random question, which she would answer, but she felt he was only asking to be polite and not because he was really interested in her life. The conversation remained one-sided for the remainder of the meal. This made it easier for Sloanne as she felt all she needed to do was nod her head and smile at Skip's little jokes.

He then ordered dessert and with it, came a change in his attitude. He seemed to become a little more nervous and began flicking the gold lighter in his hand again, but as the flame would rise, he would immediately flip it closed. It was almost like second nature to him and Sloanne did not think even he was aware he was doing it.

"I think you and I should go over to my place for a little nightcap, darlin'," Skip said smoothly.   This was what Sloanne dreaded all evening.

"I don't think that is such a good idea, Skip. I'm not the girl I used to be and I really should think about getting back home to Chloe," Sloanne replied.

"Ah, come on darlin', you know you want to spend a little alone time with me. Remember how much fun we used to have when we were alone?"

Sloanne began to be uncomfortable now. She definitely would not be going anywhere with Skip, but she was afraid to turn him down because of the circumstances.

"Maybe we could get together some other time, Skip. With all that is going on, I need to get back to Chloe," Sloanne said softly, trying to avoid making him mad.

"Damn, Chloe. I want you to myself. I have a place up the coast in Rock Hall. You'd love it. It's my little get-away place, nice and private. We could go up there and have a few drinks and maybe spend the night. Come on, Sloanne. You know you want to."

Skip was leering now and it almost made Sloanne gag.

"Sorry, Skip, but I just can't. You understand, don't you?" Sloanne said meekly.

"I understand you think you're too good for ol' Skip now. You really should be nicer to me, Sloanne. There are a lot of things I could help you with," he said and he slipped his hand into her lap and squeezed her upper thigh.

This single action nearly unnerved Sloanne. She placed her hand on his and removed it from her leg.

"Wait just a minute, Skip. I'm not your little girlfriend anymore and I'm not interested in being so again. I said 'no' and that is what I mean. Now I need to go. Thank you for the wonderful meal. Maybe we'll see each other around town before I leave," she said with conviction.

Skip's face began to get red and she could tell he was furious, but she didn't care. She refused to have him or anyone think of her as an easy piece. She picked up her bag and stood from the table. Skip jumped up at the same time and proceeded to get so close to her, she could smell the expensive alcohol he'd been consuming all evening.

"You're making a big mistake, darlin'," he whispered in her ear, but Sloanne quickly turned and headed towards the front of the restaurant and out the front door. She hurried to her car, but then she had to rummage through her bag to find the keys. By this time, Skip had made it to his car and was backing out. He pulled up at an angle that put him next to where Sloanne stood and his window came down.

"Now, darlin', let's don't end this nice evening on a bad note. I was just hoping you still felt something for me and you'd want to try to pick up where we left off," Skip said. He reached over and grabbed Sloanne's wrist as he spoke, "Come on, darlin', you played

127

hard to get and that's admirable, but now it's just you and me. Come on…last chance. Let me take you to my special place."

Skip's voice had an eerie, threatening tone now and Sloanne began to feel fear.

"Let go of my arm, Skip. You're hurting me. I'm not going with you. Just leave me alone," she said and she tried to jerk her arm from his grasp. But, he clamped down tighter on her wrist and she was sure it would leave a mark. He pulled her down until her face was level with his own.

"Who do you think you are? Nobody turns me down, bitch," Skip leered.

Just then, a couple walked out the door of the restaurant and headed towards their car. Skip released Sloanne's arm and she stood up and backed against her car door. The sinister look on Skip's face was dark and hollow with no emotion at all. Then he smiled up at her and gunned the engine of his small, navy blue Porsche, as he made his way out of the parking lot. Sloanne was really afraid now and it was all she could do to catch her breath. She was reminded of the story Chloe told her of the young girl he raped and his eyes told her that he was capable of terrible things. She jumped in her car and quickly started the engine, backing out of the space and leaving the lot. More than anything, she wanted to get away from there and back to the safety of Chloe's home.

CRUELTY TO INNOCENTS

ELEVEN

Enslaved

Danni felt searing pain rip through her and awoke with a cry. Her hands were bound behind her and the struggle she waged against the cold, steel handcuffs tore into the flesh of her wrists causing the stinging sensation of being burned. All was darkness as she tried to move, but was unable to. Her eyes were covered and no light shone through. *Was it nighttime*, she wondered? How long had she been here? Days and nights twisted together and she could no longer tell one from the other. She tried to fight the memories of the past, brutal days.

"What did I do to deserve this?" she spoke aloud.

The room was silent except for the faint sounds of distant fog horns. Danni smelled the dankness of the decaying air and she wondered if her nightmare would ever end.

She had been taken and brought here to this place. She could remember standing in the grocery store watching her mom try to help the old man. Something about seeing the man lying there on the floor made her stomach flip and she knew she was going to be sick. She turned around and ran, full speed, to the back of the store where she knew the women's restroom was. Running through the door, she barely made it to a stall before she puked. Standing there, bent over the toilet, she heard the stall door open. She remembered turning and seeing a man standing there and then feeling a small prick in her arm. Everything else was a blur. She remembered movement and light and darkness.

He treated her well at first, but as Danni's memory of the kidnapping cleared, she had become combative and he grew angry. He placed her in a machine that held her down, rendering her helpless to fight and waged war on her body. He posed her arms and legs and even told her to smile. He secured her in some type of hanging swing and did terrible things to her. No amount of begging seemed to change his course.

Danni knew about sex; she and her friends had often spoke of it in whispers and wondered what it would be like one day, but Danni also knew about the bad side of sex. Her mother often said to her when she was younger, 'Never let anyone touch you in your private places and if anyone ever does, you must tell me as soon as it happens.' Danni's mom made sure that she knew there were bad people who did terrible things to kids, but she never thought her daughter would be one of them.

When she would try to resist or cry out, he would hit her and now, not only was her body bruised and sore, but her face was swollen and beaten as well. He had done things to her she never knew could be done. Danni sobbed as she thought about how painful it had been and how she, at that moment, wanted to die. Then just as quickly as it had begun, it was over and he was gone.

He never spoke to her except to tell her to smile and she would hear a click and see a faint flash through her blindfold. She thought he must be taking her picture, but did not understand why. Sometimes he would be nice to her. He would clean her with something warm and soft and he would gently wash her hair and just as gently, brush it. He always used a shampoo that smelled like flowers. It reminded her of the smell of her street in the spring. There were always beautiful flowers there and this made her feel better and have hope.

He always fed her something warm and took great care to clean her face as she ate. It was almost like he cared about her and she could not understand what was happening. Danni would beg him to let her go, but he never spoke and would leave, only to return later angry and hurt her again.

Now, as she sat wondering about all that happened, she heard a faint shuffling sound from her left and cried out, "Is there anyone there? Pease help me."

It came to her then; the sound of whimpering...crying almost, from another corner of the room. The sounds from the darkness terrified her and she wondered if he was back to hurt her again. But the sound was not what she expected to hear. It was almost like the sounds a puppy would make, a low, soft whimper.

And then a small voice said, "Who are you? Do you know my mommy? Can you help us?"

Danni was so surprised to hear this small voice that she froze, not knowing what to think. Then she heard the small voice start to cry and call out for 'daddy'. As the voice continued, it changed. Almost like two voices in the dark. Then Danni realized there were two, small voices and she called back to them.

"What's your name?" Danni asked the voices softly.

"I'm Kimmi and my sister is Kammi. Are you an angel?" The small voice came back.

This made Danni smile for the first time in days and now all her thoughts shifted to the two, small voices in the dark.

"My name is Danni. How old are you? Are you okay?" Danni wanted to know everything at once and then realized these must be young girls, younger than she was. They sounded so scared.

"We are nine-years-old. How old are you?" came the voice.

"I'm thirteen. Are you hurt?" Danni asked again, "Can you come to me?"

"Nooo…" both voices said in unison now and Danni once again could sense the fear in them as the little voices cried softly.

Danni began to panic as she realized whoever had taken her, had taken these little girls. She also began to realize what had been done to her would also be done to them. All the terrible things she felt and had been through would soon be happening to them and the terrible realty began to set in. She grew angry.

"I'm going to help you, just try to be quiet and don't cry,"

Danni said, "Everything will be okay. Somebody is going to find us and then you'll be with your mommy and daddy."

Danni did not feel the fear now as much as she felt the anger. She wanted to hurt the person who hurt her and took these little girls away from their parents. She didn't know what she could do, but she knew she had to do something.

Just then, Danni heard the sounds of a door opening above her and she knew he was back.   Danni   whispered   to   the whimpering girls, "Listen to me, try to be very quiet and don't cry. He gets mad when you do that. I'm right here and I won't leave you, but you must try to be quiet."

"We will. Maybe he'll go away," sobbed one little voice. But Danni knew the man would not go away and she didn't say anything else, as she heard footsteps crossing the floor and the sound of keys in a lock.

She heard the creaking hinges of the door that always signaled his return and knew bad things were about to happen. She drew in a deep, ragged breath as the footsteps descended the stairs and she waited for that awful touch, but it never came. She gathered all the strength she had left and waited.

Then she heard it. The crying started again very loudly and she knew the man had gone to the little girls instead of her. Her mind raced, trying to think what to do. She could never remember being so mad and the hatred welled up, full force, inside her as the small voices continued to cry out.

"Help…Danni." She heard the cry and her mouth flew open.

"Leave them alone you piece of shit," she screamed as loud as she could. Her mind was shocked that she actually said that, but she was so mad now it had just come out. "You sick asshole, leave them alone! You're going to be sorry when the police find us. They are going to throw your sick ass in jail and you'll never get out!"

Danni was livid and she just wanted to hurl bad things at this man who hurt her so badly.

"What kind of sick freak are you? You will never get away with this and when they catch you, I hope they kill you," Danni screamed again as she heard the footsteps coming toward her and felt the tears stinging her swollen eyes.

Just then, huge hands lifted her from where she sat with one, swift motion and Danni realized she was dangling by the neck from the hand of her tormenter. Then a deep, resonating laugh sounded around her, as she felt air moving swiftly past her body, followed by sudden pain as she was smashed into a hard surface. Flashes of light danced in her mind and she felt something warm run down her neck as she gasped for breath. The squeezing at her throat was almost more than she could stand and she felt like she was going to pass out. Just then, she felt a warm body press against her length and then hot breath on her neck as the man whispered into her ear.

"Silly bitch, they'll never find you and they will never catch me," he breathed through gritted teeth.

Danni could not fight now. Her air was gone and she could only pray for it to be over.

For one second, the hand around her throat seemed to loosen and she gasped out, "I feel sorry for you."

The hand tightened again and Danni felt herself sinking into darkness. Warmth rushed over her and peace embraced her. She saw her mother's face smiling…laughing, then her friends' faces and Sloanne's. Then two small voices echoed, "Are you an angel?"

****

I picked up a few rocks I found lying around. I threw them in before I wrapped her in the heavy plastic and taped her up. *Another use for duct tape*, I thought with a chuckle. Mouthy little bitch is quiet now and I know just the place for her. I'll have to find another one. But that should not be hard and it is such an enjoyable game.

TWELVE

Simone

Simone Williams led a hard life. When she was born, her father abandoned both her and her mother, not wanting to have the added responsibility of a baby. According to her mother, Simone's father had not been much of a man in any sense of the word and her mother always said they were better off without him. Her mother drummed into her head for as long as Simone could remember, if her father was the best there was to be had, she should just think of her mother as her only parent and get on with her life. And that is what Simone did. When anyone asked about her father Simone just said she never had one…period!

Simone's mother was not much better than her father except, she was there. Her mother had been a drinker for years and when her alcoholism caused her to go through every job she managed to obtain, she turned to prostitution to pay the bills and keep a roof over their heads.

Simone's mother went through men like water. Her usual habit was to latch onto a man and move him into their house. Then, when she sucked all the money out of him she could, she would put him out and find another. The problem with this was the men her mother generally brought home were fairly shady characters, who on occasion, had done bad things to Simone when her mom wasn't around.

Simone had been abused by every sort of scum there was and one day she decided she would not take it any more. She went to school, studied hard and was one of the top students in her class. When she was old enough, she found a job washing dishes at the local diner. Once she saved enough money to afford a lawyer, she had herself emancipated from her mother and found a small apartment of her own. There were a few people in Aberdeen who had seen her struggle and offered up help of one kind or another and now Simone was attending night classes at the local community college and working days full time.

Simone was a small girl who looked much younger than her seventeen years. She was four-eleven with long, black hair, caramel skin and a very adolescent figure. To anyone who did not know her, she could easily pass for a twelve-year-old. But, when Simone spoke, her level of intelligence and maturity was apparent and surprising to those who did not know her. The contrast in Simone's intelligence and her physical size was so extreme, it prompted one of her night school instructors to suggest that she attend the Aberdeen Police Department's self defense course for women. He felt that she—being such a small person and due to the fact that she lived alone and walked most places she frequented—could only benefit from the training. So she had gone to the local Community Center and took the course. As with all her endeavors, she excelled in the training.

This particular night, Simone was leaving school headed home on foot, as usual. She was just passing the basketball courts and stopped for a minute to watch the local boys who gathered there at night to shoot hoops. She then proceeded further down the street and crossed over to the city park that was located just off campus and only a few blocks from her apartment. She cut through the park, which was her usual route and passed the gazebo in the center, working her way towards the small wooded area that lay along one edge of the park. As she entered into the dark area, she thought she heard something and stopped, but then dismissed the sound and moved on.

Just as she passed the large oak that most folks had, at one time or another, carved their name in, she heard the rustling sound again. She stopped and this time she turned around, but didn't see anyone or hear the sound repeated. By this time, she was becoming a little afraid and picked up her pace. As she hurried along she thought she heard footsteps and she took this as her queue to run, but just as she took her first stride, a large figure wrapped around her and took her to the ground hard, falling on top of her. She struggled to pull herself out from under the huge weight, but whoever was on her was much bigger than she was and she could barely move. The assailant tried to grab her arms to keep her from flailing, but as his weight shifted, Simone was able to roll her body so that she was now facing

139

up. She immediately punched upwards with her palm pointing out towards her attacker and caught him right under his nose. These actions caused the man to rear back and release her arm as he grabbed for his now bleeding nose. Simone tried to crawl backwards out from under the attacker, but now, the man seemed to double his efforts to restrain her. She kicked up with her knee and caught him in the crotch, but though it slowed him, she had not made direct contact with his testicles and therefore did not incapacitate him completely.

This seemed to further infuriate the man and he lunged at her, swinging a huge fist that connected with the left side of Simone's face and shattered the bone around her eye socket like crystal, causing her to fall backwards again. The man proceeded to punch Simone repeatedly. Every time his fist connected with her face, Simone could hear bones breaking like dry twigs. One blow caught her just below her right ear, breaking her jaw and causing her to hear a loud thrumming in her head. She fought back, pummeling with her small fists, but the man was like a wild animal, swinging again and again at her head. All during the attack, Simone had never yelled, but now, as her sight began to dim, she let out a blood-curdling scream just as the man's fist again connected with her skull.

Simone was aware now, of another sound in the distance and tried to fight again. She heard, through a painful haze, the sounds of someone yelling and her attacker jumped off her and sped away. She was not able to move or cry out again and she could feel something hard in her mouth. As she teetered on the edge of consciousness, someone else approached her and she felt hands touching her broken face. She tried to make a sound, but darkness was clouding her vision and she felt herself falling into oblivion.

****

Lamar and Anthony, two teen-aged boys who had been shooting hoops on the college court, heard what sounded like a scream and stopped dead in their tracks to listen. Not hearing the scream repeated, they ran in the direction of the sound, which seemed to be coming from somewhere inside the park just across the street. They ran toward the gazebo, as they knew this was the centermost part of the park and then, stopped to listen again.

Anthony heard what sounded like a fist connecting with a side of beef; a wet, sucking thud that the boys followed, yelling as they went. In the shadows around the big oak, they could see what looked like an animal hunched over its prey, swinging wildly. As the boys drew closer, the animal took on the shape of a man, who now spotted them approaching. Leaping to his feet, the tall figure ran wildly away from the on-rushing boys. It was then they could see the small body lying where the figure had been. As they drew closer to the body, both boys heard the sound of an engine roaring to life and the squeal of tires on asphalt. They saw a small vehicle through the break in the trees, which streaked away, but couldn't tell anything about it.

Both the boys ran up to the pitifully beaten body of a small child, but as they bent down they could tell that it was not a child, but in fact the young girl they had seen earlier watching them shoot hoops. They could tell it was her by the clothing she was wearing and they also noticed lying a few feet away, the bright green bag she had been carrying.

The girl's face was beyond recognition and although she was still breathing, blood was beginning to pool under her head from the torn flesh on her face. Lamar pulled out a cell phone and quickly dialed 9-1-1, as Anthony bent closer to the battered face of the girl. She was trying to move her mouth and he thought she must be trying to speak, but nothing came out. Suddenly, her hand flashed up and she grabbed the boy's jacket, startling him.

She weakly pulled him close to her face and in a near whisper she said, "I knooow him!"

Lamar looked over in disbelief as the girl's eyes fluttered.

"What did she say?" he asked his friend, who knelt over the girl.

"I think she said she knows him. She must be talking about whoever did this to her," Anthony said back to his friend.

Both boys stared at the girl now, not believing that this poor, battered creature was even alive, much less able to speak. Anthony, still on the ground by the girl, had no idea what to do for her so he just held onto her hand and kept repeating that the police were on their way and she was going be okay. Hearing sirens, the other boy ran out to the street to flag down the police and ambulance, which were quickly approaching the park.

As the headlights came closer, Lamar waved them towards the scene and ran ahead as the rescue vehicles mounted the curb and drove straight into the park grounds. When the body of the prone girl and the young boy kneeling beside her came into view, the police car and ambulance slammed to a stop and officers and EMTs jumped from their vehicles and headed over to the victim. Other police cars appeared and the boy waved them in also. He saw a van pull up to the curb and a tall man appear from the back with a camera swinging from his neck. The tall man ran over to the scene and began taking pictures of the battered girl as EMTs worked feverishly to stabilize her. The police commenced to cordon off the area and one officer directed both boys over to a cruiser and began to question them as to what they had seen.

"Can you boys tell me what you saw?" asked the officer, "You need to tell me everything you can remember, no matter how insignificant you think it may be. That girl is hurt badly and we need to catch the person who did this to her."

"Well, sir, we were shooting some hoops over at the college court and we heard a scream. We had seen that same girl earlier. She stopped at the fence and watched us play for a minute and then left. We've seen her before. She must go to the college because we've seen her pass by the court when we've been playing. We play there two or three nights a week," Lamar said.

"Did you see anyone else around tonight, anyone else pass by while you guys were playing?" the officer asked in a serious tone.

"No, sir. We were the last ones on the courts. All the other boys left right after the girl passed by," the boy answered.

"Do you know the other boys that were on the court with you guys? I mean, do either of you think it could have been one of them that did this?" came the officer as he wrote down the boys' words.

"I don't think so. We play with the same crew every week and most of the other guys live around here," replied Lamar.

"How old are you two? Do you live around here as well," asked the officer.

"Yes, sir. We both live just up the street. I'm seventeen and Anthony is sixteen," the boy stated. "My name is Lamar."

"What did you two see when you first came upon the scene?"

"When we heard the scream, we headed over here to the park because it seemed like this was where the sound came from. As we got to the gazebo, we stopped to listen and heard thudding sounds—kind of sickening sounds like you hear in the movies—punching sounds," Anthony chimed in now.

"Where were the sounds coming from?" the office asked.

"From the dark. Right here where we are. When we got closer, we saw a man right there, kind of hunched on the ground and

144

swinging his arms," Lamar replied. "He must have seen us because he ran off in that direction, towards the marina. That's when we saw her lying on the ground. We thought it was a kid to begin with, but as we got closer, we could tell it was the same girl who stopped at the fence."

"Did you get a look at the guy?" asked the officer.

"No, sir." said Lamar.

"How do you know it was a man?" questioned the officer.

"Because when he stood up, we could see he was big and when he ran away, he was fast. He just moved like a man. A girl doesn't move like that," replied Lamar.

"Could you tell anything else about the guy?" asked the officer.

"No. He was in the shadows the whole time, but I can tell you he was fast. I did hear an engine and see a small car hauling ass away, but I'm not sure if Anthony saw it or not. Did you, Anthony?" asked Lamar.

"Yeah, I saw it, but I can't really tell you anything about what kind of car it was. It happened too fast and the next thing I know, I was down on the ground trying to see how bad she was hurt when she grabbed my jacket. She tried to talk to me," said Anthony.

"Talk? You mean she spoke to you?" asked the officer with surprise.

"Yeah, she said 'I know him', but that's all she got out. Is she going to be okay? I mean, she's not going to die, right?" asked Anthony in a low tone.

"I don't know, but this is serious stuff here, boys. That girl is hurt and we'll need to talk to you two again. Is there anything else you can think of that you have not told me," the officer asked again.

"I don't think so," said Lamar.

"No, sir," replied Anthony.

"Okay then. I'm going to have one of the other officers take you boys home and talk to your parents. Then tomorrow, I want you two to come down to the station. We'll type up everything you've told me and we'll need you to sign your statements. You two be sure to bring your parents with you when you come. You boys have done very well tonight. If either of you think of anything else between now and tomorrow, please write it down so you don't forget. We'll add it to what we have already when you come, okay?" the officer instructed the boys.

Then the officer yelled to one of the other patrolman and asked him to take the boys home, let their parents know what was going on and instruct them to bring the boys in tomorrow to sign their statements.

"Officer Jenkins," came a voice from behind the officer who just questioned the two boys.

"Sir," replied officer Jenkins.

"Give me what you've got...the short version," said

Detective Howard who arrived on the scene and had been standing back waiting for Officer Jenkins to finish questioning the boys.

Detective Howard had been with the Aberdeen Police force for a little over eighteen years and he was beginning to think the town of Aberdeen had been cursed. For as long as he could remember, there had never been this amount of crime in the area. He wondered what the heck was going on and why things changed so much. He loved his work, but he never had to deal with these sorts of crimes here before. That was one of the reasons he took the detective position. But now, with the kidnappings and people being beaten on the streets, he didn't know how much longer he wanted to continue in this line of work.

Howard, with his blue-eyed glint, brawny looks and cocky 'tough-guy' stance was a no-nonsense detective, who saw the facts for what they were and believed only what he saw. He was a formidable man of six-foot, who could easily intimidate with a glance and he often used that to his advantage when necessary.

"They didn't see much. They think it was a man who attacked her because he was tall and ran away fast. They couldn't really tell much more about him. They saw him run in the direction of the marina and heard and saw a small car speed away, but no make or color. That's about it. I'm beginning to think this guy is a ghost, Detective," said the officer.

"I hardly think there's a ghost anywhere around here that

could have done this to that girl. But I am wondering if this could be connected with the kidnappings. She is a really small girl. ID says her name is Simone Williams, black, four-eleven and ninety eight pounds. Maybe whoever did this thought she was younger. Hell, she looks like a ten-year-old. The guy must have been desperate or psychotic to beat someone like that. EMT says she's in a coma and they are rushing her to the hospital. He said her injuries were pretty extensive and she may not make it," replied Detective Howard.

"The girl spoke to one of the boys before she passed out. She said 'I know him'. Maybe if she comes out of it, she can identify the perp," replied the officer.

"She spoke to one of them after going through that beating? She must be a tough kid. We'll just have to wait and hope she comes out of it. Until then, we need to keep a lid on this. People are already freaked out about these kidnappings. If this gets out, this town will be in an uproar. Make out your report and then give it to me. I want to talk to those two boys myself when they come in tomorrow. Make it happen," said Detective Howard. "Also, I need you to get on the wire and see if you can locate a next-of-kin for the girl and let me know. In the mean time, I'm going to talk to Birney Sullivan and see if I can get him to sit on this story until late tomorrow."

"You got it, sir."

With that, the officer turned and walked back over to his cruiser and left. Detective Howard lit a cigarette and took a few puffs. Then he snubbed it out and walked over to the cordoned off area.

"You guys find anything interesting," he asked the forensics tech.

"There's a lot of blood around. The girl must have fought back. There are some marks on the ground here that indicate a struggle. She must have been dragged or was trying to crawl away from the perp. There are some foot prints leading off towards the marina and we'll get a cast of those. They look to be about a size twelve, but I'll check for sure back at the lab. I directed the EMT to have the ER swab the girls nails and I'll collect whatever they find later. I'm still checking this area and it will take a while to get everything. I'll write up what I have when I'm done and get it to you as soon as possible," replied the tech.

"Okay then, put a rush on this one. I need to know what's happening here and I need to know now," replied Detective Howard.

"I'm on it, Detective. I'll put this one on the front burner and get you what I can, but it may take a few weeks for DNA tests," replied the tech.

"I'm aware of the time frames. Just get going on it," huffed Detective Howard.

He then turned and looked around for Birney Sullivan. He didn't have to look far. Birney was just the other side of the cordoned off area, trying to get information out of one of the other officers. Howard walked around the area and tapped Birney on the shoulder just as he was starting to put his finger in the officer's face. Birney stopped mid-sentence and turned to Howard.

"Look, Sullivan," Howard began, "I don't want any of this story getting out just yet. You know how people in this town are and if this gets out, we're going to have a bigger mess on our hands than we already do. With the kidnappings and now this, people are going to be afraid to send their kids to school. You understand, right?"

"I understand the people have a right to know what's going on in their town. The police need to be taking care of the citizens around here and you guys don't seem to be doing a very good job of it at the moment," sneered Birney.

"Look, Birney," Howard smoothly replied as he rested his hand on Birney's shoulder, "I'm not asking you to kill the story completely, just give us a few hours to see what we can come up with before you let it break. That's all I'm asking. We are doing everything we can right now. At least give us until late tomorrow afternoon. If we don't find anything substantial by then, you can run with it. But people are getting scared and we don't need a panic situation here."

Birney Sullivan worried that his scoop would get stolen right out from under him, but he understood where the detective was coming from. He thought maybe this would work to his advantage, so he formed a plan.

"Okay, but I get exclusive rights to this story. You don't talk to anybody else from the media except me," Birney bargained.

"Now, Birney, you know I can't do that. But I'll make a deal with you. How about I call you first with whatever we find? I'll even agree to let you ask the first questions when this story breaks to the media. Will that suit you?" Howard replied.

"Deal. Now I need to get back and get rolling on these pictures. You call me tomorrow afternoon about four and let me know the status of the case. If you don't call, these pictures will be on the front page of the late edition," Birney said.

"I'll call, Sullivan. You just make sure you keep a lid on this," Detective Howard retorted.

He wondered if Birney would be true to his word. But then he thought better about it. He made deals like this with the man before and he never reneged in the past.

Detective Howard turned back to his car and walked the distance, thinking about all he knew. He opened his door and just as he slid into the driver's seat, his radio squawked. He picked up the microphone and pressed the button.

"Howard here. Speak to me," he said.

"Detective Howard, Jenkins here. I ran a check on the girl's identification. Seems she has been emancipated for about a year. She works at the diner, goes to school nights and lives alone. Her mother is her only kin, but I haven't gotten a line on her yet. She may be going by a different name than the girl, but I'll keep checking. Anything else you want me to follow up on?"

"Damn, not much is it? See what else you come up with and keep me posted. I'll be in to the station house in a bit. I'm going to ride around the neighborhood and see if I see any suspicious cars in the area," replied Howard.

"Copy, out," and the radio went quiet.

Detective Howard cranked his car and lit a cigarette. As he pulled off the park green, he was thinking about everything that was going on in his little town. After eighteen years of police work, his instincts told him things in Aberdeen were about to get very nasty. After today, nothing would be the same.

THIRTEEN

Fishing

Bill Ingsley was a retired machinist turned charter boat captain. He had been working the Chesapeake Bay for about ten years as owner/operator of Double 'D' Fishing Adventures, a day-charter boat business.

Bill was born and raised in the South, but had gotten tired of the hot, southern summers and decided to move north. Since he complained most of his life that he'd rather be fishing, he decided to fish for a living. He moved to Havre de Grace Maryland, sinking almost all his retirement money into a forty-foot Morgan with a pair of 320HP turbo, diesel engines and started his business. It was slow at first and Bill worried he'd made a bad move, but soon the charter business caught on and the customers and the money rolled in. Word got out that Bill was a southern man and soon the southerners came in droves. Bill spent all his days doing what he loved best, except now, he was getting paid to do it.

Bill was a big man, standing six-four and weighing in at two hundred twenty-six pounds. He had long, strawberry blond hair that was going to gray and he kept it pulled back in a pony tail most of the time. He had steel-blue eyes and didn't smile much, but he was considered a cutter who liked to joke and make others laugh. The index finger on Bill's right hand was missing down to the first joint

153

and he always told the kids he lost it to a rambunctious bass, but he actually cut it off while working in a machine shop. Bill liked his beer, but he never mixed fishing and drinking. He figured the customers on his boat could drink enough to cover him.

The day started out as normally as any other day. Bill made a quick run-through with his mate, Daryl, checking supplies as usual. They checked bait amounts, tackle, fuel levels, food supplies and also performed the USCG required equipment checks. The day's charter consisted of five business men from north Mississippi who were attending a paper company convention in Baltimore. Two of the guys had been out with Bill before, but the other three were rookies and Bill was interested to see what the day would bring.

The men were supposed to be ready to leave the dock at 7 a.m., but started arriving about 6:30 a.m. The guys Bill knew showed up first and the others followed shortly behind. After loading the men and their gear, Bill started the engines and let them idle for a few minutes while everyone got situated and comfortable. Bill then maneuvered the forty-footer out of the City Yacht Basin and into the boat channel at a point where the Susquehanna River emptied into the Chesapeake Bay.

Just as they passed the Fishing Battery Lighthouse heading south into the bay, Bill saw some shading on his fish finder and decided it would be a good spot to wet a few hooks. The charter group all set to preparing lines with Bill and Daryl helping each in

154

turn with whatever they needed.

Everybody settled in to do some fishing and time drifted by. The guys seemed content and Bill found himself enjoying the day. As time went along, a few rock fish were caught and as noon approached, Bill started thinking about feeding the passengers.

Just as Bill stood to head to his make-shift galley, one of the guys called out, "I got a big one over here," and he proceeded to try to reel it in.

He was having some trouble with the fish and Daryl began to help the man with the obviously large catch, which had not yet broken the water.

"Captain Bill, better get the gaff. By the feel of it, dude's got himself a wall-hanger," Daryl yelled over to Bill.

The other guys started whooping and yelling. Bill smiled as he thought about the first big one he caught in these waters and he knew this would be a day his customers would never forget.

Just as Bill grabbed the gaff pole and stepped to the gunwale, the catch hit the top of the water, but something just didn't seem right. Bill and Daryl must have had the same thought because they looked at each other and then back in the direction of whatever had attached itself to the end of this man's line. This was no fish.

"What do you think that is, Captain?" Daryl asked with a perplexed tone.

"I don't know, Daryl. Maybe it's a body," Bill said with a

smile. The entire charter group chuckled at Bill's joke, but Bill was not sure what he was looking at wasn't really a body. As quickly as the thought crossed his mind, Bill dismissed it as an impossibility and looked over at Daryl and said, "Come on, Daryl. It's probably somebody's idea of a joke, just a fish wrapped in plastic and thrown in the bay. Pull it up. We need to get the hook out at any rate."

Bill commanded and handed Daryl the gaff pole. Daryl moved the gaff pole over the object and then jerked up hard on the handle, impaling it with the sharp point of the gaff. He pulled up, but the object was obviously heavy. Bill reached over the gunwale as Daryl lifted and grabbed the object at one end, heaving it over the railing and onto the deck, where it landed with a thud. The object was torpedo-shaped, wrapped in heavy plastic that was secured with duct tape.

One of the charter group said, "If that's a fish, it's a mighty big one."

Bill was starting to wonder what the hell was lying on his deck. He thought maybe it was somebody's dope that had gotten lost overboard. He heard there were drug runners in these waters, but had never run across any in his time. He assumed anything was possible these days. Hell, for all he knew, it could be something worth a ton of money and he didn't want to get left out of finding a stash of cash or some ancient treasure. But then again, maybe it was a body. Bill shivered slightly.

"Should we open it, Captain?" Daryl asked, but the look on his face said he didn't want to be the one who slit the plastic.

"No, Daryl. I think we better just call the marina and tell them what we've got. I'll have them call the police and send someone to meet us at the dock. We'll let those guys handle this. I don't think I want to have any part of what's wrapped in that plastic," Bill replied. He then turned to the charter group, "Sorry guys, but I think we need to get back to the marina and let the police take over whatever this is. I will give all you guys a voucher for a free day of fishing and refund your money for today. How does that sound?"

"I pretty much agree with you, Bill," said one of the guys Bill knew and the others chimed in with agreement. They helped the passengers reel in all their gear and then turned the 'Double D' back towards the marina. The suspicious bundle lay on the deck and everyone's eyes seemed to keep coming back to the spot where it rested. Quiet had fallen on everyone as they raced back towards the marina. Bill got on his radio and spoke to the harbor master, telling him what transpired and that he should call the police and have someone meet them at the dock.

As they approached the marina, the dock came up fast and just as the boat came alongside, Daryl jumped over to secure the line. Bill cut the engines and headed to the gunwale just as the man Bill knew as the harbor master and a sheriff's deputy, stepped onto his boat.

"Whatcha got, Bill?" asked the harbor master.

Bill motioned to the bundle on the deck. Both of the men's faces took on a look of surprise and then dread. The deputy walked around the bundle and then stooped down trying to get a better look. It was almost like he was hoping he could see inside the bundle from a lower angle, but he could tell nothing else about the contents.

"I think I better call the sheriff and maybe the coroner before we slice into this," declared the deputy. "Would you guys mind lifting it out of the boat and setting it on the dock?"

Bill and Daryl gave each other a pained look, but Bill knew the thing had to come off his boat so he said, "Come on, Daryl. Let's get this over with."

They stepped over to the bundle and each took an end, lifting it and swinging it over the gunwale. They both seemed to sense something and gently set the bundle down on the dock.

The party stood around for a few minutes waiting for the sheriff and coroner. Ten minutes later the sheriff arrived and stepping out of his car strode up the dock to the group of men.

"This better be good, Deputy, you dragged me away from my lunch for this," boomed the Sheriff, as he eyed the bundle, "If you boys have brought up a bundle of trash it's not going to sit well with me, I can guarantee that."

"I don't know what it is, Sheriff, but it looks mighty

158

suspicious," said the deputy in reply.

"Ah, hell boy. Cut the damn thing open so I can get back to my meal."

"But the coroner is on his way, Sheriff. Don't you want to wait until he gets here?"

"You called the coroner? Damn fool. Cut that plastic open now or you'll be handing out parking tickets by tomorrow," the Sheriff bellowed.

The deputy reached in his pocket and pulled out a Swiss army knife, flipping open the blade. He slipped the blade into one end of the bundle and slit the plastic up about a foot. He withdrew the blade and then peeled the plastic back. The site that greeted the onlookers was gruesome. A small foot with painted pink toenails fell from between the folds of the plastic.

The group of men had been standing around waiting to see exactly what they dragged onto the dock and now two of the men gagged and one quickly dropped to his knees and puked into the water. The other men could only stare in disbelief at what they saw before them.

Bill stepped back from the gruesome sight and said, "Fuck! What the holy hell is going on here?"

The Sheriff instantly jumped back from the bundle in horror and without saying a word, turned and ran down the dock to his cruiser. Snatching the microphone from his radio, he first made contact with the coroner, who was just turning in the gate to the marina. He then radioed the station house and requested four more deputies be sent to the scene. He walked back to the dock and instructed the passengers not to leave and no one was to touch the body any further or disturb it in any way.

Bill could not believe this was actually happening. All he could see in his head was the sight of the small foot peeking out from under the plastic and all he could think of was, *pink is my granddaughter's favorite color*. The size of the foot told him it had to be a young girl or a child and he kept seeing his granddaughter's face. He stood there shaking his head as if doing so would erase from his mind, the site of what was lying on the dock. Why would anyone do this to another human being?

The sheriff told the group of men on the dock they all needed to find a seat somewhere and relax. He wanted to question them all regarding the mornings find and as soon as the extra men arrived, he'd have them set about doing just that. He was apprehensive as to what the coroner would say about him ordering the deputy to slit open the plastic. He was aware that some kids had been kidnapped in Aberdeen and he figured maybe this was one of them, but he didn't say it out loud. He just kept quiet now and everyone waited.

First to show up was the coroner, followed by the requested deputies. Then, Detective Howard from the Aberdeen Police drove up. He had a man with him the sheriff thought he recognized, but he couldn't place how he knew the guy. Next, a van from the *Aberdeen Chronicle* rolled up. Birney Sullivan jumped out and came up the dock, but the Sheriff stopped him before he could take any pictures. The coroner was already bent over the body and the deputies were over questioning the charter group about what transpired.

"Hold up on those pictures, will you, Birney? At least give the coroner a chance to see what's what before you get in his face," the sheriff said to Birney who was chomping at the bit to get some good shots.

"You need to let me pass, Sheriff. You know I'm the press and people need to know what's going on. Too much stuff is happening around here lately and folks are getting scared. Now you fish up a body. I just can't keep a lid on this anymore. I heard this on the scanner and I'm sure other people did too. You can bet they are going to want to know what's going on," replied Birney just as Detective Howard and the other man walked up.

"Afternoon Sheriff...Birney," said Detective Howard, "Sheriff, this is Patrick Louchlin. He's a retired New York City detective who has been helping us on the kidnapping cases. We heard over the scanner that you pulled up a body. Can you give me any other details?"

"Yeah, I'm familiar with Mr. Louchlin. My department buys some supplies from your business, I believe, sir," the sheriff replied, extending his hand to Patty.

"All we know right now is there is a body in that plastic. My deputy slit the end open and a small foot with pink-painted toenails fell out. Damndest thing I've ever seen. I know you boys have some kids missing in your town. You thinking this could be one of them?"

"At this point, it's an unfortunate possibility," replied Howard. "We have three girls missing and no leads to speak of. There has been no ransom request and we are at a dead end. Then we heard about this over the scanner. Mr. Louchlin and I need to get a look at that body. We have pictures of the missing girls and we really need to identify and hopefully eliminate this body as one of them."

"Howard, we made a deal last night, but this changes everything. I just can't sit on this story any longer. If you want to give me a statement, I will try to quote you, but people need to know about this for safety's sake, if nothing else. Whoever is taking these kids is serious and the more people know, the better," Birney piped in now with urgency.

"Now wait a minute, Birney. We don't know that whoever took those kids is the same person who dumped this body or beat that girl last night in the park. These incidences may not even be related. At least let us get a look at the body to see if it is one of the kidnapped kids before you go full out with this," pleaded Detective Howard.

"Sorry. I just can't go along with you on this anymore,

Howard. You're right, these cases may not be related. Problem is, you boys don't know one way or the other. I got a job to do here and people have a right to protect themselves. My editor has already threatened to fire me if I don't get this story in the late edition and that is what I intend to do. Now, I'm going to get pictures of this scene and if you guys can come up with anything in the next two hours, you know how to contact me. Excuse me." Birney replied as he stepped back and began to take pictures of the chaos unfolding on the dock.

Bill Ingsley came up the dock, headed for his boat. The deputies finished questioning the charter group and let them go and Bill was going to move his boat to his slip and clean her up a bit. As he met the group standing on the dock he stopped.

"Bad day to fish, I guess," he said to no one in particular.

"You're right there, Bill. Hopefully, no more of your charters will be fishing up bodies. Sorry it had to happen," the sheriff said.

"Better today than tomorrow. Got a Baptist church group from Kentucky coming. Imagine them making today's catch?" Bill replied, trying to lighten the mood. He then turned and walked to his boat.

FOURTEEN

Telling

By this time the coroner loaded the bundled body onto a stretcher and was about to wheel it toward the shore. He had been careful not to disturb the plastic any more than necessary to get it loaded. Normally, Jack Parsons, the forensic guy for Harford County, would have come out to the scene and taken over the body himself, but his wife picked today, of all days, to have a baby and he was stuck at the hospital. The coroner agreed to take the chain of evidence upon himself and get this body off the dock and back to the lab. Jack promised to meet him there in an hour. Detective Howard was approaching him and he knew what the man wanted before he opened his mouth.

"Now, Howard, I can't let you see this body until the forensics man opens this up and does his evidence gathering and you know it, so don't even ask," the coroner said. "If you boys want to follow me to the lab and wait, I'm sure Jack will let you get a look at it as quickly as he can, but I'm responsible for it right now and I say, *no.*"

Detective Howard just nodded to the coroner and then turned to Patty.

"I guess we have no choice at this point, Louchlin. We'll follow them in and wait until the forensics man gives the go-ahead. I suppose another hour or so will not make that much difference, at least not to whomever is wrapped in that plastic. I surely hope it's not one of those kids, but I can't help but believe it is, since there have been no clues and no ransom requests."

Howard noticed the somber expression clouding Patrick Louchlin's face, but they were all feeling somber now. He hated the fact that somebody was kidnapping kids in his jurisdiction or anywhere for that matter. But if this body turned out to be one of those kids, he would *have* to believe these terrible things were happening here.

"I'm afraid to see who that is in there," Louchlin replied to Howard.

"If it is one of those little girls, there are going to be a lot of very sad people in Aberdeen. My goddaughter and her best friend being two of them. I don't know how I'm going to break this to them. They are still trying to be hopeful that things will turn out well. This is going to be a blow to them even if it's not their Danni. Damn!" Patty groaned as he passed his hand over his brow.

The two men followed the coroner and his charge down the pier and to the waiting ambulance. Howard helped the coroner load the body and then he and Louchlin got in their car and followed closely to the forensic lab in Bel Air. Bel Air was the county seat of Harford County Maryland and where the sheriff's department, government offices, coroner and forensics lab were based.

The two men were quiet as they rode along, following behind the ambulance with its light flashing, but no siren, an indication that there was a non-emergency transport in progress. The drive to Bel Air took about twenty-five minutes, but seemed much longer to Patty.

He considered calling Sloanne to tell her of the new development and give her time to prepare herself to give Chloe the news. He could not decide what the best course was if this turned out to be one of the kids that had been taken. If it was Danni, Patty knew that Sloanne and Chloe would be devastated. If it turned out the body was not Danni, but one of the other children, it would almost be worse. Chloe and Sloanne would be thinking that if the kidnapper killed one child, he would probably kill them all. Either way, this was a bad situation and Patty was not sure what he should do next.

"Louchlin, we're here," Detective Howard's voice came to Patty and roused him out of his train of thought.

The ambulance was pulled into the parking bay, indicating that the coroner already unloaded the body and moved the vehicle. Detective Howard and Patty walked through the double doors and into the forensic waiting area. Through the window they could see Jack Parsons talking to the coroner. He glanced towards the two men and nodded. The men stood in the waiting area for what seemed like an hour, but was only fifteen minutes. The coroner then came out to the waiting area and addressed the two men.

"Jack is going to go over the outside of that plastic and then he'll cut it open. As soon as he does, he'll call you two back and you can get a look at the body. Dirty business, this," he gestured in the direction of the autopsy room and continued, "I'm glad I'm not the one who has to contact the family. I'm going back to my office and write my report. It should be ready before you guys leave here if you want to get a copy," the coroner told the two men.

Detective Howard thanked the man and he turned and left.

"What do you think is happening here, Howard? We have never had crime like this around here before. Aberdeen has been a quiet, safe place to live for as long as I've been here. It's starting to feel like the big city now."

"You're right there, Louchlin. You've seen this type of crime in New York before, right? Me? I've never worked anywhere but right in Aberdeen and I just don't get it. I can only assume that these crimes are being committed by some out-of-towner or a drifter passing through the area. We just don't have people living around here that are capable of doing this sick shit."

"I guess you can never be too sure who lives in your community and what kind of person they really are. Monsters can hide in the most open places. Hell, you can know someone for years and never really know what goes on in their head. I have learned not to take anything for granted when it comes to police work," replied Patty.

"I guess you're right, but I'd like to believe that if somebody like this crossed my path, I'd have some idea about how sick they were before they had a chance to hurt anybody," Howard replied.

"These sick types don't have something stamped across their forehead so we recognize them. Whoever did this could be somebody you talk to every day. The lady at the grocery store, your kid's teacher, the high school football coach, the preacher at your church, anybody! People can have evil in them and never even know it themselves until something happens to bring it out and by then, it's too late and the damage is done," Patty mused almost to himself.

"Damn, Louchlin, jaded much?" said Howard with a shrug. "Your time in the city must have been pretty illuminating. You seem to have seen the worst in humanity."

"Yes. But I've seen the best too. Kind of evens the scales, I think."

The two men sat in silence as time passed slowly.

Finally, Jack walked through the door and towards the two men.

"I hope this is not one of the kids you're looking for. She's pretty beat up and looks to have been assaulted. You boys can come back and take a look and I'll give you what I have so far," the forensics man said to them both.

The three men proceeded to the back and through a door marked 'Autopsy'. The smell assailed their noses, but being police, they smelled it before. There was a stainless steel table in the middle of the room connected to a sink and a long counter. A large surgical light hung over the table and there was an x-ray machine on an overhead transom that carried it back and forth to be adjusted as needed. There were counters around the perimeter of the room with all manner of equipment laid out for use by the coroner and forensic people. Only one wall was reserved for the cold storage of bodies with several roll out drawers to accommodate them. On the table lay the plastic bundle, opened down the middle with the plastic pulled back.

As the men approached the table they could not tell anything about the body in the plastic, but as they drew closer, there lay the badly beaten body of Danielle Jacobs.

Howard and Louchlin both shook their heads and looked away as Jack Parsons began to tell them what he found on preliminary inspection of the girl.

"Is this one of the girls who was taken?" asked Jack.

"Yeah, that's Danielle Jacobs. She was the first girl taken a little over a week ago. Can you tell how long she's been dead?" Howard asked.

"The body looks to have been in the water for about twelve to eighteen hours, give or take. And I believe she was killed within the past twenty-four hours and dumped in the water. I found these flat rocks wrapped in the plastic with the body. Whoever did this,

169

weighed her down. If you look closely around this area on her neck, you'll see what looks like a large hand print. The cause of death was probably strangulation. She also has some petechial hemorrhaging in the eyes and on several other locations on her body. Lots of bruising and some weird marks on her wrists and ankles. They look like some form of restraint was used, but I'm not sure about that yet. She also has bruising on the back of her feet as if she was kicking with her heels. You can see the shape she's in. Must have taken a lot of beating and there are defensive wounds on her arms, so she fought back. There is also this puncture wound on her side, but I believe that may be where the guys fished her body out of the water. I'll have to do a complete autopsy, x-rays, blood analysis and rape kit. We'll check her for prints and residual DNA that shouldn't be there. This is going to take some time boys, but at least we know what happened to one of your kidnapped kids. Let's just hope we don't find anymore like this one," Jack finished reading what he had so far and closed the file he was holding. Looking back at the two men, he added, "There's one more thing. I have a buddy who works for the Oceanographic Center in Boston. I'm going to give him a call. They have buoys in the bay and they can chart currents, water temperature and wind speed. Maybe if I can give him a time-of-death, he can give me an idea about where she may have drifted from. It's a long shot, but maybe it will help us."

"We appreciate your help, Jack. You know how to get in

touch with me whenever you find out anything definitive," Howard said.

Both he and Patty shook hands with Jack and turned to leave.

"You two have the hard job now—telling this girl's mother about what's happened to her. I'd rather do my job any day," Jack said half-heartedly.

Both men nodded and walked away.

The two headed to the car and Howard stopped. Lighting a cigarette, he drew in hard and let out a long sigh, exhaling the smoke.

"Well, Patty, now what?" Howard said sighing again, "How do you want to handle this?"

"I think I need to give Sloanne the news. She's is going to have to be there when Chloe is told. Poor woman is going to lose it. That girl was her only family. This is really going to rip Sloanne up too, but she'll do what needs to be done for Chloe and for Danni. She's a strong person and I know she'll know the right thing to say. I can't do this without her there to help," Patty said with anguish in his voice.

He pulled out his cell phone and stared at it for a moment before dialing Sloanne's cell number.

As he waited for Sloanne to pick up, he thought about what had to be done and felt responsible for not having done enough to prevent this tragedy. Danni had been a beautiful child and no one should have to suffer as she did. He was determined to make things right.

"Hey, Patty," Sloanne answered on the third ring.

"Hey, kiddo. Where are you?" Patty asked in a somber tone.

"We're at Shawn's apartment. We just got back from the firehouse search party. We were up looking around the Proving Grounds, but nobody spotted anything. What's up? You sound down," Sloanne inquired nervously.

"What's the address there, kiddo? I got some things I need to talk to you about in private."

"It's 125 Applewood Lane, apartment B. Is something wrong?" Sloanne asked.

"We'll talk when I get there, okay? Be there in a few," with that Patty hung up the phone and got in the car with Detective Howard.

He relayed the address and Howard started the engine and headed to Shawn Tyler's apartment.

****

"That was Patty?" Shawn asked.

"Yes, he's coming over to talk. He sounded like something was wrong, but didn't want to talk on the phone. He didn't even say goodbye. Just hung up. That's not like him. Something is really wrong," Sloanne said, her voice sounding frightened now.

"Now, Sloanne. Let's don't jump too soon. He's under a lot

of stress too. We all are. Would you mind making some coffee while I change? Patty will probably want some when he gets here too," Shawn said, leaning in and placing his hand on Sloanne's face and then turned to go change. Sloanne figured Shawn was probably right, so she headed for the kitchen and started looking for the makings for coffee. She put everything on a tray and carried it out to the living room. She put the tray on the coffee table just about the time Shawn walked back into the room. Sloanne heard the sound of two car doors slamming and wondered who Patty brought with him. She tensed as a knock came at the door. Shawn threw her a reassuring smile and headed over to open it.

There stood Patty with Detective Howard. Both men looked drawn and Patty never made eye contact with Sloanne. She knew right away something was terribly wrong.

"Tell me," was all Sloanne could say and the look on Patty's face told the worst.

Sloanne's knees went weak and she thought she might fall before she realized Shawn was by her side. Patty stepped towards Sloanne, but she stopped him with her outstretched hand.

"You tell me now. Say it! Where is Danni?" Sloanne demanded.

"Sloanne...her body was found in the bay this morning around 11 a.m. The coroner has her and they are trying to find out what happened. I'm sorry. It looks like she was strangled. I don't think you need to hear a lot of details. I'm sorry, kiddo. We did our best, but it just wasn't enough," Patty said in a low, calm voice.

Sloanne backed away from Shawn and Patty. Her head came up and a scream came out of her that was more anger than heartache. Her fists shook at her side and she gritted her teeth. Squeezing her eyes shut, she remembered all the times that Danni smiled and laughed. She could hear Danni's voice and she remembered all the wonderful talks they had, all the silly phone calls just to say hello, all the trips to New York they enjoyed together. All this was gone. Sloanne began to cry. She thought of all the things Danni would never be able to do. She'd never go to prom, never have her first boyfriend and never fall in love. There would never be that phone call from Danni saying she was graduating from college or she was getting married. Danni would never have children and Chloe would never get to hold her grandchild. Sloanne stepped to the sofa and eased herself down. She stared at the floor for several minutes before she spoke, "How am I going to tell Chloe?"

Shawn stepped over to Sloanne and took her hand in his, "I will be there to help you. We'll tell her together."

"We'll all be there for Chloe and I'll be here for you," Patty said as he stepped to Sloanne and took her other hand.

Sloanne's mind was in shambles. She was in more pain than she'd ever thought possible, but she knew they needed to go and break the news to Chloe. She remembered the pain of her parents' deaths, but this was different. She remembered her mother saying once that no parent should ever have to bury their own child and now her best friend would have to bury her daughter. She had no idea if Chloe would be able to recover from this, but she would stay with her as long as she needed. Nothing else mattered right now. She willed herself to stop crying and wiped her face, determined to be strong for Chloe and to see this whole ordeal through to the end. She would make sure whoever did this to Danni would pay. Even if it took a lifetime, she would make sure Danni's death did not go unpunished. She thought about the other children who were missing and she immediately turned to look at Shawn. His face was a mask and she knew he was thinking about his nieces too.

"We have to find Kimmi and Kammi and we have to do it quickly before something terrible happens again," Sloanne said to the group, but she was looking at Shawn.

"The window we are working with now is getting smaller as time ticks by. Seeing Danni and the shape she was in, I can't help but believe the girl who was beaten in the park last night was this guy's next, intended victim. She was just too hard to grab and now he'll be looking for another kid to snatch," Detective Howard said with unease.

"What girl in the park? What are you talking about?" Shawn said, shocked by this new revelation.

"There was a girl beaten last night in City Park. Two young

boys came on the scene and scared the perp away, but not before he did a number on the girl. We think she saw the guy and can identify him, but she's in a coma now. We hope she makes it through and can give us a description at some point," replied Howard.

"Jesus! You mean to tell me that not only is there someone kidnapping kids, but now he's going around beating girls too? And killing them?"

Shawn's hands went to his face and then through his hair. A sure sign of his stress level. Sloanne knew he was thinking about his nieces and wondered if they were still alive. This case was turning into a monster and she knew they had to do something quickly before another child was murdered.

"Now hold on a minute. This just doesn't make any sense. It doesn't match this guy's MO. Patty, you know the statistics on these people. They rarely, if ever, stray from their established pattern. Why do you think this beating is related to the kidnappings?" Sloanne asked both men, now stepping into the roll of law enforcement.

"To be honest with you, it was just a hunch…a feeling I had. But after seeing Danielle, I feel almost certain the two incidences are related. The girl who was beaten in the park was small in stature, leading me to think our perp may have mistaken her for a younger girl. I believe he was planning to kidnap her, but she fought back. That's why she ended up getting beaten so badly. Her fighting back probably pissed the guy off and he just snapped. He's got to be psychotic," said Detective Howard.

"After hearing the details on Ms Williams and seeing the shape that Danni was in, I'm inclined to agree with you on this. A town this size, with little or no crime and suddenly, these horrendous things are happening. I've got to think all this is related and this guy is now a loose cannon. These cases may have started as kidnappings, but now it has escalated to rape, torture and murder. This is our guy. I can feel it and he's making some pretty big mistakes. I only hope we can be there before the next mistake is another murdered child," Patty explained.

Sloanne was feeling worse than ever now. She was now realizing how much Danni must have suffered before her death. She could tell from what Howard and Patty said that Danni's body was in bad shape and that she had been raped. Sloanne kept seeing her poor Danni in her mind and the visions were devastating. She also thought about Shawn and what he must be thinking and her heart nearly split in two. She was devastated for herself and for Chloe and she felt so bad for Shawn and his family. No one should have to go through this. She knew Shawn's brother and sister-in-law were frantic about their kids and when they learned about Danni, they would be hysterical. If she were in their position, she didn't know if she would be able to survive.

Sloanne then looked at Patty and she saw a strangeness there on his face, that she had never seen before. The look in his eyes, a set to his mouth…something she could not recognize and she wondered what he was thinking. Was he holding something back from them? And if so, why?

Her mind was so scattered from everything that happened, she could barely think at all. All these new facts where weighing on her and she just wanted to stop thinking. Her mind went to Chloe and she knew the next thing she had to do was to go to her friend and tell her that her only daughter was dead.

"We need to go to Chloe's *right now* and tell her about Danni before she sees it on the news," Sloanne said quietly.

"Yes, we do. Birney Sullivan was at the dock and he'll be letting this story drop any minute," Howard added.

"You're right. Sloanne and I will go over in my truck. I know she'll have to be with Chloe, but at some point, I'll need to go to Ed's to give them the details too. This is going to kill them," Shawn said.

His hands kept going to his hair and Sloanne could tell he really didn't know what to do. His mind was muddled by everything that was happening and he was afraid for his brother's family…his family.

"We'll follow you over there. I think it's best if we're all there when you tell Chloe. She may or may not have questions, but we need to be there in case she does," Patty said.

Sloanne stood and collected her bag. Shawn made sure he had his keys and Detective Howard and Patty headed towards the door. Sloanne turned and looked at Shawn and he could only look at her and shake his head.

"I'm so sorry, Shawn," Sloanne whispered to him. "I'm sorry for your family. I wish you could have been spared all this. I wish we all could,"

"None of us deserve this. We just have to figure out who this is and stop him. Those girls are depending on us. We couldn't help Danni and now she's gone. Maybe we can get to Kimmi and Kammi before this guy hurts them. I want to believe we can. But right now, we need to get to Chloe. I'll be there with you for as long as it takes. Then we have to find out who this guy is and nail him," Shawn said with determination.

Sloanne nodded and they both walked out the door. Detective Howard and Patty were already in their car and Sloanne and Shawn got into his truck to follow them to Chloe's.

Sloanne didn't know how she would break the news to Chloe, but it was a short ride to her home and she resigned herself to be as honest and straight- forward as she could be with her best friend. Sloanne steeled herself to the inevitable: Chloe would be devastated and she knew this single act would be the hardest thing she ever had to do. She took a deep breath and waited as they drove to Chloe's. Shawn reached over and took her hand and just held it, as if he knew what she was thinking. It gave her a feeling of comfort and safety. She knew she had to be Chloe's rock now, but Shawn was turning out to be hers and that was a surprise. Who would have ever guessed she would find anything but sadness in this town?

Both vehicles pulled up in front of Chloe's house at the same time. Patty stepped out of the car first and came to open Sloanne's door. As he took her hand, they heard the sound of Chloe's front door opening. Sloanne took a deep breath and looked towards the door and into the eyes of her best friend. Chloe's normally, brave face immediately turned to bitter sorrow as one by one she panned the faces of the approaching group. She knew the worst immediately, just as Sloanne had when Patty and Detective Howard stood at Shawn's door. Chloe instinctively knew her daughter was gone. She took one step and began to beg, "No...please! She's okay...she's coming home. Tell me she's okay, Sloanne! You tell me my baby is okay. Please! Please! Oh God, please tell me my baby girl is coming home!"

And with that, Chloe fell to her knees and let out a wail that Sloanne could feel to her very soul. She ran to her friend and went down beside her and wrapped her arms around her while Chloe prayed to God to bring her baby home. But, her prayers would not be answered and Sloanne didn't think she could help her friend at all. She didn't know if she could even help herself. The two women held each other and cried there on the front stoop and the three men stood around them in anguished silence. Patty's hand was on Chloe's shoulder as if his touch could somehow make things better. Shawn reached out to Sloanne, but then his hand just dropped to his side and his head went down to his chest.

Sloanne let Chloe cry, it was all she could do. After a few minutes, Sloanne tried to stand and help Chloe to her feet, but she could barely see through her own tears. Shawn stepped in to help Chloe stand, but she seemed unable to move, so he scooped her up into his arms and carried her into the living room. He gently set her down on the sofa and Sloanne was right there beside her, quickly embracing her again as she sobbed uncontrollably. Patty and Detective Howard stood in the foyer, but neither said a word. They were all at a loss to console this inconsolable woman. Patty went toward the kitchen thinking he would make coffee. He didn't really want any, but thought maybe someone would eventually. It would get him away from the intense sorrow that filled the room. Detective Howard turned and went out the front door thinking now would be a good time to make a call to the station house in case anything new had come up.

Sloanne held Chloe and they simply rocked and cried together on the sofa for what seemed like an eternity. Shawn was there, right in front of them, kneeling on the floor. There were still pictures strewn across the coffee table and he couldn't help but look at the smiling face of Danni Jacobs staring back at him from the reminders of happier times. He reached up and wiped his face and felt the moisture of tears he had not even been aware he shed and he felt more sorrow than he knew was possible.

As Patty walked back in from the kitchen he noticed the TV was on, but the sound was muted. He could see there was a report running about Danni's body being found and he hoped Chloe did not look up and view the scene. From the looks of it, a reporter from the local TV affiliate had gone to the dock to do a story on the gruesome discovery. With the dock in the background, the reporter was obviously telling the story of the fishing group pulling up the body and bringing it in to shore. He wondered if the reporter knew who the body belonged to or if she was telling the local viewers her theories as to whether or not the body belonged to one of the kidnapped children.

Just as Patty's eyes flashed to Sloanne and Chloe still rocking on the sofa, Shawn saw his face and looked in the direction of the TV to see what caused the stressful expression Patty now wore. As Shawn realized what he was seeing, he looked to Patty and then slowly eased up from his position in front of the sofa, stepped back and pressed the 'off' button on the TV and headed towards the front door. He went around Patty, who at once recognized the look on Shawn's face as tension and followed him out the front door.

"I've got to get over to Ed and Gwen's. They have probably already seen that news cast and are beside themselves. I don't want to leave Sloanne, but I have to go to my family," Shawn said with anguish.

Detective Howard stepped up and said, "I'll go with you, Shawn. Maybe I can help you. I'm sure your brother and his wife will have questions. I know they will be upset and I don't know what else I can do here."

"I'll stay here with Sloanne and Chloe, Shawn. I know Sloanne will understand why you had to leave. Don't worry. Just come back as soon as you can, please. Sloanne is going to need all the moral support you can give her. Chloe will never be the same after this. She will probably want to see Danni's body and I don't know how I will handle that. I'd rather she not see her. No mother should have to see her child in the state that Danni is in. Just get back when you can," Patty said, placing his hand on Shawn's shoulder.

Shawn turned away to leave and then turned back to Patty.

"Tell Sloanne that I—tell her I'll be back as soon as I can, please," Shawn said sadly.

Patty looked at Shawn and could only nod.

FIFTEEN

Demons

It took the coroner four days to release Danni's body. The police performed every test imaginable and gathered all the information they could. Those four days were like a horrible nightmare no one could wake from. The police requested the next-of-kin do a positive identification, but Chloe asked that Sloanne go in her stead.

When the coroner revealed the mangled and distorted body of Danni, Sloanne stood for a long moment in shock before uttering the words, "Yes, that's Danni". She was thankful Chloe wasn't there. Sloanne knew the image of Danni's slain body would have haunted her mother forever.

Chloe slid down into a deep abyss of grief and remained there for some time. Sloanne did not know how to help her mentally, but tried to do whatever was physically necessary to ease her pain. She would not eat or drink, and when she spoke, it was in a confused, soft whisper. Sloanne spoke to Chloe's doctor and he suggested they try to get her on some medication, so he wrote a prescription that Shawn picked up from the local pharmacy and brought over.

Shawn had his own family turmoil to deal with, but helped with Chloe every chance he had. His presence was constant and he

184

was the most solid entity in Sloanne's life during those terrible days. She knew his bother and sister-in-law were frantic and he was doing all he could to console them as well. It was nearly impossible to console the parents of a missing child, especially in this situation. Since Danni's body was found, Gwen slipped into a deep depression and Ed didn't know what to do to help her. Shawn did his best, but all this weight was beginning to take a toll on him as well.

Sloanne was forced into the roll Chloe was unable to assume and all responsibility fell on her to give Danni the memorial and burial she deserved. Sloanne visited the funeral home and spent hours going over the arrangements with them. She picked out the outfit Danni would be buried in and the picture to be displayed beside her closed coffin. She spoke with friends and accepted gifts of food and condolences from neighbors and strangers alike. It seemed everyone in the area heard about Danni and all wanted to let Chloe know she was not alone.

During those times when Chloe was resting and the house was quiet, sadness and grief would close in around Sloanne. The despair she felt was unimaginable and she cried many times when she was alone. She missed Danni and missed the family that Danni and Chloe were to her. She knew things would never be the same again and felt so helpless to do anything for her friend. She felt grief before, but this time it seemed different. Maybe because the life cut short was that of someone so young or because she knew Danni suffered. The fact that someone made Danni suffer in the worst possible way was the hardest part for her to accept. She knew it was a fact and would have to come to terms with it, but Chloe probably never would. Sloanne knew something had to be done and intended to make sure the person who killed Danni would pay for it.

It was during these dark times she tried her best to push the feelings aside and focus on researching all the information they gathered. She looked into cold cases with the same MOs as this one. She felt whoever performed these terrible acts had possibly done them before in another place or time. Every deed was executed so cleanly and with such precision she could not believe whoever was taking these children, had not done this before. She knew the police were doing everything possible to track this kidnapper, but felt if she second guessed everything they did, maybe she could find a clue they missed. She knew Patty was working day and night along with Detective Howard, but still felt an extra set of eyes may be able to turn up something new.

In her research she came across a case in New York City from over twenty years ago which was similar in some ways. She recalled her parents discussing a case her father was working involving the taking of children. It was about the same time that her father was shot in the line of duty and retired. She remembered snippets of their conversation and could hear her father saying it just didn't pay to help people anymore. She was a young child at the time and dismissed it as 'grown-up talk'. She thought back to what she could remember of their conversation and wondered if there was any significance. She made a mental note to ask Patty about it. She knew he would remember any cases they worked together. She also remembered her father kept records on some of the more involved cases he worked. She assumed those records were in the attic of the house her parents lived in before their deaths—the house she hadn't been to since returning to Aberdeen. As much as she hated the idea of going there, she figured she should go by and see what she could dig up.

Shawn went to the newspaper office and picked up all the newspaper articles published so far on the case and they spent hours reading and re-reading everything they gathered. Looking at the newspaper photos, searching for any clue the police may have missed, they made lists of similarities and talked about the case constantly, trying to see something there they had not seen before. They were both trying to keep their minds occupied and away from the grief and sorrow felt for themselves and for Chloe and Shawn's family.

Sloanne felt closer to Shawn than to anyone during those days and she could tell he felt the same. He was kind and gentle with her and she knew he was a person she would always be able to depend on. She knew they were growing closer and believed at some point, they would become involved on a much deeper level. She knew that time would have to be in the future. Right now, they were both determined to find the missing children and the person who was taking them.

On the fourth day as Shawn and Sloanne were again scouring over the newspaper articles, they heard a door open upstairs and shortly thereafter Chloe appeared in the living room. She looked haggard and tired, but something in her eyes had changed. Sloanne believed she crossed over that line between extreme grief into acceptance. She walked over to the sofa and stood, looking at the vast array of collected information Shawn and Sloanne amassed. She seemed to be taking in certain pieces of some of the articles and pictures that were strewn around.

"So where are we? Have you found anything the police might have missed?" Chloe asked tiredly.

Sloanne stared at her for what seemed like minutes, but amounted to only seconds before she spoke again.

"Sloanne, you always had a second sight when it came to this type of work. You always look at things differently from most people and your instincts are always spot-on. I knew you would throw yourself into finding the monster who took Danni. What have you come up with?" Chloe asked with determination.

Sloanne gave her a smile because she knew Chloe was back and determined to catch this killer. Chloe's new-found strength bolstered them both and they began telling Chloe everything they knew about the case so far.

"We have come across a couple of things. I don't know if they have any significance in this case or not, but it is a start," Sloanne said.

Shawn jumped into the conversation then.

"Sloanne dug up an old cold-case file from New York in which kids were disappearing from accident scenes. On the surface everything appears the same, but we haven't gotten enough detail to know for sure if this could be a link to our case. Sloanne thinks maybe her dad kept some files and we're going to go over there and check in the attic to see if we can find anything."

Chloe gave Sloanne a worried look. She knew how much Sloanne dreaded going to her parents' home. She had not been there since their deaths and Chloe knew how difficult making the trip would be.

"How do you feel about going over there? I want to go with you, I need to help now," Chloe said to Sloanne.

"I would do just about anything for Danni and for those girls. Kimmi and Kammi are still out there somewhere. We need to do whatever is necessary to bring them home. If it means I have to face my demons, well so be it," Sloanne said to Chloe.

"If you can go, then I can go too. I'll get dressed and be back in five minutes," Chloe said turning to go upstairs, but then turned back to Sloanne.

"Thank you, Sloanne. I know how hard this has been on you. You have no idea how much you have meant to me and to Danni," with that, Chloe turned and ran up the stairs to change.

Ten minutes later they were in Shawn's truck heading for Sloanne's parents' home. Sloanne pushed aside the negative memories and tried to concentrate on the here-and-now. Chloe asked questions about the case and Sloanne tried to answer everything she asked. The route took them through the neighborhood where Shawn lived and as they approached an intersection the girls both looked down the street towards Shawn's duplex and saw the same thing at the same time.

"Sloanne?" Chloe started.

"I know. I see it," she replied.

"See what? Did I miss something?" Shawn asked inquisitively.

"The king-of-creeps is parked outside your place," Chloe said dramatically, shivering for emphasis.

"What? Who? What are you two talking about?" Shawn asked with confusion in his voice.

"Skip Perryman is parked outside your house," Sloanne replied.

"Why the hell would Skip Perryman be parked in front of my house. I'm not his type!" Shawn said with a grin.

"I think he may be looking for me. But how did he possibly

find out about you?" Sloanne asked.

"You forget where you are, Sloanne. This is Aberdeen and everybody knows everything about everyone here," Chloe said with sarcasm in her voice.

"Okay. I give. Why would he be looking for you in the first place? I know you guys were involved in high school, but that was then and this is now so what's the deal?" Shawn asked.

"Skip still has the hots for Sloanne and apparently he's not only a creep, but he's taken up stalking as well," Chloe spat out.

"He cornered me in town the other day and threatened to have his mother withdraw the Perryman's financial support for the search unless I agreed to have dinner with him. I went along, but he really creeped me out and now I have to admit I'm a little afraid of him. He has changed a lot since school," she explained.

"Changed a lot is an understatement. I hear he had his share of run-ins with the law and his sexual tastes run to the criminal side. His mom managed to get him out of a rather sticky situation with an under-aged girl in college and it wouldn't surprise me if mommy's money got him out of several situations. I hear he is fairly kinky with the women. He's become eccentric and people say he's even bought some property over in Rock Hall where he takes women. I hope I'm not overstepping my bounds when I say, I would appreciate it if you'd stay the hell away from him, Sloanne. I'd hate to have to hurt the old boy," Shawn said as he clenched his teeth.

"Okay. I can take care of myself, Mr. Macho, but I appreciate your concern," she said with a wink.

Sloanne was afraid of Skip and didn't mind if Shawn looked out for her. In fact, she rather liked the idea. Just then, she recognized they were on her street and dread pushed everything out of her mind.

They pulled up in the driveway of her parents' house and got out. Sloanne fished in her pocket for the key to the front door and hesitantly walked up the porch steps. The place looked the same except a little more weathered than the last time she was here. She slid the key in the lock and turned the knob. The door swung open and as she stepped inside, a wave of relief washed over her—just the way coming home should feel. Surprising as that feeling was, she was glad for it. Chloe and Shawn followed her through the door and they all stepped into the living room. Chloe began to wander around the room looking at the pictures while Shawn just glanced around with awe.

"Who read all these books?" Shawn asked as his eyes took in the rows of tightly- packed bookshelves lining the walls of her parent's living room.

"My dad and I did. He loved books and reading and I guess it rubbed off on me. I forgot how many books there were until now. He bought them everywhere he went. Mom used to make fun of him about bringing them home all the time."

192

Sloanne smiled as she explained her dad's obsession.

"No wonder you're so damn smart," Shawn said with that cocky grin.

Sloanne just smiled as she ran her fingers over the old volumes lining one shelf.

"Funny. Look at this Sloanne—cops and robbers," Chloe said, passing her an old frame.

It contained a picture of them as kids playing the game they loved best. Sloanne as the good guy and Chloe, as always, playing the bad guy.

"This is a great house, Sloanne. Lots of care taken with the place and I can tell that love lived here," Shawn said smiling to himself.

"I think it still does. I thought coming here was going to be hard to take, but now I wish I'd come sooner. It feels like my parents are still here—comfortable—you know?" she remarked quietly.

"It does to me too. It even smells the same, like wonderful old books. There's even that smell of lavender in the air. Can you smell it, Sloanne? Your mom loved lavender," Chloe said with a slight grin.

"I guess we should start in the attic and work our way down. I'm sure if my dad kept his old records, the attic would be the place to store them," Sloanne said and headed for the stairs. Shawn and Chloe followed close behind and they made their way up the steps.

The foyer at the top of the stairway was also lined with bookshelves and again Shawn's eyes were taking in everything. Just at the far end of the area was a small doorway that hid the stairway up to the attic. They walked up the stairs single-file and stepped onto the attic landing.

Along one whole wall of the attic area were shelves filled with labeled boxes containing the records her father kept. She never realized he collected this much information and as they began reading the labels, she realized her father was a meticulous record keeper. Everything was alphabetically arranged and completely labeled with dates and contents of each box. She was amazed at the time her father took to do all this work, but it didn't surprise her. He believed in his work and in doing things right and here was the proof.

"What year are we looking for again?" Chloe asked as she perused the shelves.

"I would say between 1984 and 1986," Sloanne replied as she checked dates on several boxes.

"Got it. Right here."

Shawn called from one end of the attic. He slid a box off the shelf and headed towards a large desk situated in the center of the attic.

"There are a couple more boxes back there with this same date. I'll bring them over," he said as he turned to head back to the line of shelves.

Chloe turned on the two lamps sitting on the desk while Sloanne slid over three chairs.

Sloanne tipped the lid off the first box and tossed it to the floor by the desk. Inside were several discolored file folders. Each one bore a date, case number and disposition of the case. Shawn walked up with the other two boxes and set them down by the desk. He sat down, grabbed a few of the folders and began to go through them. Chloe was engrossed in her own stack by then and Sloanne decided they would probably need to take some notes. She stood up and went back down the attic stairs to her second-floor bedroom to find a pad and some pens. Coming up empty handed, she went down the stairs to the kitchen, knowing that her mom had always kept pens and paper there for the lists she made.

She started back through the living room and passed the front window. She saw a glint of sunlight reflected off the super-shiny exterior of Skip Perryman's Porsche, which was slowly passing in front of the house. The chills that went up her spine were nearly as unnerving as the sight of Skip staring at the front of the house as he drove slowly by. She stopped at the window and watched as his car passed from view and then something began to nag at her—the small car he was driving. A small car had been seen leaving the shopping center when Danni was taken. A small car was seen when Simone Williams was beaten. The tire tread in the grocery store parking lot was foreign in make. She kept running the facts through her brain as she climbed back up the stairs to the attic. She knew where this thinking was taking her. She wondered how Skip could possibly be involved in all this. *Why would he be? He had all the advantages life could offer—money, position, power—everything. Maybe all that wasn't enough.*

"Sloanne. We found something. Where are you?" Chloe yelled from the attic landing.

Sloanne blanked as she bolted up the stairs to see what they found.

"Here they are. Five child abductions between 1984 and 1986. All unsolved and Sloanne, none of these kids were ever found. Your dad and Patty worked this case for two years before your dad was shot and retired. What do you think?" Chloe asked solemnly.

"What other details are in there?" Sloanne asked.

"There are a few more details about the kids, but this looks so much like our case, it's uncanny. Your dad must have worked this case in his off-time. There are a lot of notes in the margins about the kids being taken from scenes of accidents. Here's one from a robbery. A shooting victim was being helped by a doctor who just picked up his daughter from a ballet studio next to the crime scene. The daughter was taken while the man helped the victim. They never found her. This is just too close to our guy. Have you talked to Patty about these old cases?" Shawn asked.

"No. I intended to, but he's been so busy, I haven't had a chance. Now that we have this information, I'm sure he will be able to tell us more. We need to get a look at the crime lab photos of Danni's body. Patty can help us with that," Sloanne said as she looked to Chloe's sad face.

She knew if there were any similarities in the file Patty would be able to pass them along to the forensic people for comparison to Danni's case. She also knew that Chloe did not know the details and the amount of suffering Danni endured. She felt it was too soon for her to know everything that happened to Danni. Sloanne did not want her slipping back into that dark place again.

As if she had read Sloanne's thoughts Chloe said, "I think I'll run downstairs and see if I can scare up something for us to drink. Be right back," and with that, she was gone.

"I'm afraid she will want to see the pictures of Danni," Shawn said in a low tone as he handed Sloanne the pages from the file.

"I think she read my mind. I'm glad she knows her own limits. I don't think she could handle the real story about Danni's death at this point. I don't want her in any more pain," Sloanne replied.

Sloanne tensed as she looked through the files. It was almost more than she could take. Here were five more children whose parents lost the most precious thing in their lives. They woke up one morning happy and by day's end their worlds were turned upside down.

Chloe soon returned and they all went through the boxes. They segregated the files on the abduction case, but did not find any other cases that matched their own. After several hours in the attic, Chloe began to look tired. Shawn packed up what they found and the group headed back to Chloe's.

Tomorrow was Danni's memorial service and there were still loose ends that needed to be tied up. Sloanne made sure Chloe ate and was resting before she made a call to Patty. He spoke with Jack Parsons, who promised to messenger over the forensic photos of Danni's body. After some persuasion, Sloanne convinced Patty to allow them to view the photos and to keep her in the loop on the investigation. Patty would drop the photos by Shawn's house later that day so Shawn left heading home to be there when the file arrived.

After Chloe fell asleep, Sloanne proceeded to make sure they're clothing was laid out for Danni's funeral in the morning.

This would be the hardest part of the nightmare and she wondered how Chloe would hold up. She questioned how she would hold up as well. She faced some of her demons today and tomorrow, Chloe would face her own. They would face them together as they always had.

CRUELTY TO INNOCENTS

SIXTEEN

Memorial

Originally, plans for Danni's funeral service had been schedule at the small chapel where Chloe and Danni attended church, but due to the immense outpouring of support from the community, the funeral director urged Sloanne to forgo the smaller chapel and move the service to St. Michael Vincent, the largest church in Aberdeen

St. Michael's was the most beautiful cathedral-style church in the area. The large church entrance consisted of huge, dramatic double doors that appeared immovable, due to their enormous size. They led into a massive, elaborate sanctuary with stained glass windows depicting beautiful, biblical portrayals adorning all sides. The sheer height of the clock and bell tower was neck-breaking to view. Beautiful, angelic music could be heard playing from the tower at clock strike and the church was a county-wide landmark.

Chloe and Sloanne arrived at the church at 10 a.m. and were ushered inside by the funeral director. They were taken to a small, elaborate room behind the sanctuary where Danni's coffin was resting. Sloanne knew that Chloe did not want to see Danni. They had discussed this earlier in the morning and Chloe had agreed that she would rather remember Danni as she was. Sloanne suspected that her friend had a good idea of what Danni had gone through in the end and she knew Chloe would not be able to look at the remains of the daughter she loved. The funeral director asked if they would like a few moments with Danni's coffin opened to them and they both quietly said no.

Chloe and Sloanne approached the coffin solemnly. Chloe's face was so sad, but she smiled at the memory of her lovely daughter. She mumbled a few words of love for her child and then laid a kiss on the coffin. Sloanne also laid her hand on Danni's coffin and then said her goodbyes.

The priest entered and stood beside Chloe and Sloanne. They said a prayer together and he commented on what a great loss her passing was to the community. The body of Danielle Jacobs would never be seen by another person and her sweet voice would forever be silent. But, Sloanne could hear Danni and she intended Danni's cries for justice would not go unanswered.

As Sloanne and Chloe returned to the sanctuary and sat in the assigned pews, they noticed for the first time the vast sea of flowers surrounding the pulpit and the place where Danni's coffin would stand. Sloanne was amazed at the outpouring of love and sympathy from the community and she felt the impact Danni's passing had on everyone.

The church began to fill and Danni's coffin was wheeled into the sanctuary and was delicately set in its place amongst the flowers. So many people were filing in and taking their seats. Sloanne saw

Shawn arrive with Ed and Gwen and they made their way to a pew right behind her and Chloe. Shawn leaned over the pew and placed his hand on Sloanne's shoulder. He bent down and placed a kiss on her cheek just as Chloe looked up and smiled at him. He then placed his hand on Chloe's shoulder and sat down. Ed's hand took the place of Shawn's on Chloe's shoulder and he whispered his condolences and asked Chloe how she was doing. She reached up for his hand and gave him a small smile to reassure him, but that was all she could manage.

Sloanne saw Patty enter the church and walk the distance to the front where they were sitting. He entered the pew where Sloanne and Chloe were seated and sat next to Chloe. He gently took her hand and kissed it and then smiled at Sloanne. Several of Aberdeen's finest entered in full dress uniform and lined the church walls. Sloanne saw the Perryman's enter and sit towards the back of the church. Skip immediately spotted Sloanne, but never looked directly at her, keeping his head low and his eyes downcast. Rochelle and John held their heads high as always.

The crowds continued to enter and at one point, the funeral director approached Sloanne to tell her a PA system had been set up to accommodate the people who were still arriving and would have to remain outside due to lack of seating. Sloanne was amazed at the volume of people who came to Danni's funeral. Finally the priest entered the sanctuary and the crowd quieted to hear his words.

"We have come together to morn the untimely passing of Danielle Jacobs. I did not know Danielle personally, but from the number of people here today, I believe she must have been an exceptionally lovely child and her passage into the house of our Lord does not go unnoticed by many people in this community. Of course, Danielle will be missed by her family and closest friends, but I feel she will be missed by all who came into contact with her in her short life. She is with God now and she will dwell with him forever. Her Mother's best friend and Danni's godmother, Sloanne Kelly would like to say a few words about Danni and what she meant to her. Sloanne, would you come up?" the priest asked in a humbled voice.

Sloanne got up and walked to the pulpit to face the crowd of people.

"Danielle Jacobs was not just a picture on a flyer or a tragic story on the news. She was not the sum of her ending in this life. She was my family. She gave with all her heart to all who sought her and she loved with a trueness, beauty and warmth that even the wisest failed to grasp. She was a friend to many and never looked to someone for what they had, but rather what they had in their heart. Danielle was a daughter and her mother will forever feel the void that has been left by her passing. Danielle was a dreamer, who believed she would one day change the world through her writing. She often said words could change the world and one person can always make a difference. I believe Danielle has made a difference in the life of every person she ever came into contact with. I know we are all better for having known her. I was not there when God delivered her into this world and I was not there when she walked from it back into his arms. It is a darker place here without her, but Heaven is so much brighter with her there. I miss you Danni, I love you, sweetheart. I will see you again one day," Sloanne ended as she lifted her head to the crowd. Tears poured down her face, but she was not alone. Every eye in the building was full of pain and sorrow for Danni's passing. Shawn stood and hurried to Sloanne's side to escort her back to her seat, his arm around her protectively and lovingly. He again placed a kiss on her cheek as she sat down by Chloe and the priest returned to the pulpit.

He proceeded to read Psalms 23-25 and then read the funeral mass. Prayers where said and responses made by the congregation. The priest then stated graveside services would be held at St. Michael's cemetery and then the force of officers from the Aberdeen Police Department filed past Sloanne and Chloe to take Danni's coffin from the church. They filed out of the church lifting the casket into the back of a hearse as Sloanne and Chloe stood on the church steps watching the procession.

All the people began to file out of the church, each giving their condolences to Chloe and Sloanne. Patty and Detective Howard were standing behind Sloanne. Shawn, Ed and Gwen walked out of the church too and were standing with Patty. Shawn moved to

Sloanne's side and stood quietly there with her. Many people filed past, taking Chloe's or Sloanne's hand and saying words of hope and apology for their loss. Sloanne was still amazed at the number of people who had come to the service and she also was grateful to Patty for the show of police she knew he initiated. They made a difficult situation just a little more tolerable and she knew Chloe was proud of her beautiful daughter and would remember, always the impact her life had on the community.

Just as Sloanne was about to lead Chloe down the steps to the waiting limo, the Perryman's appeared in front of them like an omen from hell.

John Perryman stepped up to Sloanne and Chloe and shook both their hands in turn and then stood aside. Skip stood a few steps behind his parents and never came forward. He stood glaring at Shawn. Sloanne wondered what was going through his mind as his eyes met hers. The look on his face was unreadable and Sloanne could not fathom his thoughts at all. Then Rochelle stepped up to Sloanne and Chloe.

"Sloanne, dear. The service was quite lovely. Who knew you could deliver such a moving eulogy," Rochelle cooed.

"Thank you, Rochelle. It was not meant as a eulogy, but my last words to Danni," Sloanne said in an even tone. She refused to let Rochelle get to her…not today.

"Of course, dear. And you, Ms Jacobs, how horrible for you.

What you must be going through. How are you holding up?" Rochelle's voice was as smooth as glass.

"I'm doing my best, thank you, Mrs. Perryman," Chloe mumbled.

"I just can't imagine the guilt you must be feeling. I could hardly live with myself if I were in your shoes," Rochelle's venom rolled from her mouth.

"Guilt? Guilt over what, Rochelle? What are you implying?" Sloanne spat at the woman.

She could not believe Rochelle said that to her friend and the Irish was beginning to surface in Sloanne.

"I simply meant, if you had been paying more attention to your own child instead of trying to help some stranger, she might still be here with you," Rochelle oozed out.

Sloanne took one look at the tears that popped into Chloe's eyes and it was all she could take. All the bad feelings she ever had towards Rochelle Perryman now drained into Sloanne's right fist and she cocked Rochelle on the jaw as hard as she possibly could, knocking the woman on her privileged ass, right there on the steps of St. Michael's church.

Sloanne then bent down to Rochelle and politely said, "Screw you, bitch!"

The look on Rochelle's face was one Sloanne would remember her whole life and she nearly burst out laughing. Chloe made a choking sound and Sloanne looked up to see a large grin behind the hand Chloe put to her mouth. A muffled chuckle came from Patty and Detective Howard and Shawn's eyes took on an obviously amused look. Not one person reached to help Rochelle Perryman get to her feet including her, always-gentlemanly husband, John.

Rochelle was so flustered trying to stand that she slipped down again. She then began to protest loudly that Sloanne assaulted her and demanded the officers standing nearby should arrest Sloanne at once. Each man in turn then looked to the next, but none moved to help Rochelle or seize Sloanne.

Patty stepped forward and looked down at Rochelle, who was still on the ground.

"Madam, I fail to see what you are talking about. No one here has assaulted you as far as I can tell. You must have slipped on the concrete."

With that, Patty turned and walked down the steps ushering Sloanne and Chloe along with him. Shawn, Ed and Gwen proceeded right behind them. As Sloanne looked back up the stairs, she noticed that John and Skip finally came to Rochelle's aid and were helping her up from the steps. She watched Rochelle with a satisfied smile as they all got into the limo and left for the cemetery.

SEVENTEEN

Messenger

Sloanne felt drained from the funeral, the altercation with Rochelle and the grave-side service. She knew that Chloe had to be as tired and drained as she was. Shawn was taking them home and Sloanne intended Chloe rest. She was sure neighbors would be showing up bringing food and more condolences, but she did not believe Chloe could handle much more. Shawn received the crime lab photos from Patty late the day before and after dropping off the girls, he planned to go retrieve them. Even though Sloanne was tired, she was anxious to see the photos. She asked Patty to come by later and gave him a short run-down of what they found in her father's files. Patty seemed a bit distant, but she put that off to everything that was going on.

As they pulled up to Chloe's house, Sloanne saw a limo parked across the street and a tall man immediately got out as they pulled in the drive. He walked up the sidewalk and addressed Sloanne directly.

"I am trying to contact Miss Sloanne Mae Kelly. Would that be you?" asked the man in a decidedly British accent.

"I'm Sloanne Kelly. How can I help you?" Sloanne replied.

"My name is Walter Pagent and I represent the estate of Mr.

Philippe Miera. I need to speak with you on an urgent matter. Can we go inside and talk?" the man asked.

"Of course we can talk, but what do you mean by 'Estate of Mr. Miera'? Has something happened to him?" Sloanne asked urgently.

"Let's please go inside and I will explain everything to you," replied Mr. Pagent.

She felt a familiar rise of panic, but proceeded to show Mr. Pagent into Chloe's house and directed him to be seated in the living room while she quickly made coffee for them. Shawn came into the kitchen and asked if she wanted him to stay. She thought a minute, but was anxious to see the photos he had at his apartment, so she asked him to go ahead and get them. Chloe was upstairs and after Shawn left, Sloanne ran up quickly to see if she needed anything before she lay down. She urged Sloanne to attend to the gentleman downstairs and told her to be sure to call if she was needed.

Sloanne readied the tray of coffee and took it into the living room. She placed the tray on the coffee table and seated herself opposite Mr. Pagent.

"Now, please tell me what is going on with Mr. Miera," Sloanne said.

Immediately, Mr. Pagent began to delve into a briefcase at his side. He pulled out a laptop and placed it on the table in front of Sloanne, opened it and pressed a button. Sloanne did not speak, but simply sat quietly. Within seconds, an image popped onto the screen and Mr. Miera's warm smile could be seen. Sloanne smiled back as if he were really in front of her. Mr. Miera began to speak directly to Sloanne.

"Hello, my child. I hope you are well. Sadly, if you are watching this, I am no longer with you."   Sloanne's heart sank in her chest and she felt sadness rushing over her again. Her long-time friend and mentor was gone.

"You know I have no family of my own, but if I would have had a daughter, I'd have wanted her to be just like you. I have always seen so much of myself as a youth, in you and I always believed you would do great things with your opportunities and with my company. You know I think of you as my own child and I have always wanted the best for you. With that being said, I have made arrangements for you and my company. I have always believed you would make your mark on the world, but not necessarily as an interior designer. I know, however, you will make the right decisions for Miera Architecture and put the right people in positions of authority. I know you will insure my business and my name live on, long after I am gone. Therefore, I have left the controlling interests in Miera Architecture to you and also a large sum of money. Mr. Pagent will explain all the details to you. I hope you will use the money to find your true calling in life and be happy. Please, my girl, don't cry for me. I have lived a good life and I lovingly leave what I have built to the one person I trust the most. I love you, my girl! Please be happy as I am now. Goodbye, Sloanne."

Sloanne couldn't be sad for the old man. He asked her not to be and she would honor his wishes as she always did. He was her rock at a time when she'd needed one and she would be the best she could be now, for him. All this was so mind-numbing and she had so many questions for Mr. Pagent.

"What happened to Mr. Miera? What did he die from? Why would he leave me everything? I'm not even kin to him. We were very close, but I never expected this. Please tell me what is going on, Mr. Pagent."

The questions poured out of Sloanne. She was so upset about her mentor, but amazed at this turn of events. She didn't know what to make of all this.

"Mr. Miera was suffering from a condition known as Marfan syndrome. It is a fairly common genetic disease. He has had it since birth and there is a fifty percent chance of passing the disease on to children. Hence, why he never married. He has been taking medication for years and should have had surgery many times, but he always felt it wasn't the right time to be ill and therefore he never was. At least not to anyone who knew him. He never wanted to be seen as a sick man and never wanted to be fussed over. So, he felt it was best if those closest to him did not know about his disease. He passed away from an aortic rupture in his sleep and it was a peaceful passing. By his request, he was quietly cremated and his ashes were spread out over part of his estate in Ireland. He has a castle there, by the way."

Mr. Pagent opened his mouth to begin again, but by this time Sloanne was overwhelmed. She threw up her hands in a gesture for Mr. Pagent to stop.

"This is so overwhelming. I can't believe Mr. Miera was ever sick a day in his life. He seemed so robust and healthy as long as I have known him. How could he have ever been so sick and I never knew?" Sloanne poured out.

"The alcoholism he suffered from when you two met surely did not help his condition. He never wanted you to know and he was a wonderful actor," Mr. Pagent replied in a kind voice.

"I just can't believe he is gone. What am I going to do without him?" Sloanne breathed, almost to herself.

"Miss Kelly, I imagine you will be able to do whatever in life, you want to do. You are an extremely wealthy woman now. The board members of Miera Architecture are all aware of Mr. Miera's decision and have been for quite some time. They are all in agreement with the provisions he has laid out and have given their word, no decisions regarding the future of Miera Architecture will be made until you have tied up your loose ends here in Aberdeen and are available to meet with them in New York. Mr. Miera has also left you a short list of individuals working within the company, whom he believes honest and quite capable of taking on leadership positions within the company, in the event you are unable or unwilling to take on the role yourself. Mr. Miera has also placed a clause in his will which states, if you chose to place another in the role of CEO, you have the option to sell your shares to the other board members. However, fourteen percent of shares will be retained in your name for the lifespan of the company. There is also a large sum of money involved, Miss Kelly," Mr. Pagent continued.

"Wait! More money? What do you classify as '*large*', Mr. Pagent?" Sloanne inquired, bewildered by all this.

"Roughly $37.7 million in cash," Mr. Pagent said, almost nonchalantly.

Sloanne ran her hand through her hair and then consciously had to close her mouth. She was unable to even grasp the sum this man was presenting her with. Was this really happening? Sloanne did not believe things like this ever happened and now here she was being told she was wealthy. She found herself looking around for someone to jump out at her with a camera. This was unbelievable and yet it was reality.

"Mr. Miera has also put into place, the necessary provisions with his accounting firm and they are prepared to help guide you in dealing with such a sudden and astronomical windfall. There is also his estate, which includes his home and its contents, several automobiles and all the property. Aside from the rare books and

213

artwork, Mr. Miera has graciously made arrangements to have all these things sold at auction, with all proceeds going to *The American Heart Association*. The books and artwork are yours to do with as you wish. There is also one other thing, Miss Kelly."

"More? How could there possibly be more?" Sloanne stuttered out.

"The castle and surrounding estate in Ireland…they now belong to you. Mr. Miera has left you specific instructions not to sell this property and to quickly make provisions in your will to insure this property stays in your family indefinitely. I will be more than happy to help you draw something up, Miss," stated Mr. Pagent.

"I don't know what to say or how to process all this. I am so sorry that Mr. Miera has passed. He was such a good person and he cared for and helped me through so much. I will miss him terribly," Sloanne was still floored by this whole revelation.

"I do have a few documents for you to read over and sign so that I may get things rolling along, but in the mean time, I have a cashier's check to see you through until all the paperwork is concluded. It is a meager sum, but I believe you will be able to mange for a time."

With this, Mr. Pagent handed Sloanne a check. Her hands shook as she accepted it and as she looked at the amount, her jaw dropped open again.

"You consider this 'meager'? Mr. Pagent, I don't know if I

can accept this? I don't...." Sloanne stammered as she looked at all the zeros on the check.

"You can and must. This is not a gift. It rightfully belongs to you and it is a fulfillment of Mr. Miera's request. I can't leave here until you accept this check. Please, Miss Kelly, I know you are shocked, but you must believe that Mr. Miera had your best interests at heart and he wanted you to have all he has left you. You are a very lucky, young woman. I knew Mr. Miera for years and he placed you above all others. You should be very honored by all this," Mr. Pagent began shuffling papers and pulling out what he would be leaving with her.

"I am very grateful to Mr. Miera and I will try to live up to what he expects from me and for his company. I will try to make him proud."

"I assure you, Miss Kelly, you have already made him proud and I am sure you will do the best thing for his company. I am at your disposal whenever you need me as Mr. Miera has retained me for the life of his estate," Mr. Pagent said pulling out a business card.

"You're saying I have inherited your services as well?" Sloanne asked.

"But, of course. Mr. Miera was very meticulous and my firm has represented him for years. He paid us handsomely for our services and we are forever indebted to him. I am now available to you at the drop of a hat, Miss Kelly. Please feel free to call me at any turn, day or night," and with that he handed Sloanne the card with his business numbers and web addresses as well as his personal contact numbers.

Sloanne felt like she just stepped out of an old episode of *The Millionaire*. She took the card and the papers that Mr. Pagent placed in a simple folder.

"I will need for you to sign these two documents now. The first is a simply-worded contract that states you wish my firm to continue to represent you in this and all further matters pertaining to the estate. You, of course, have the option of retaining your own legal counsel after the estate has been officially awarded to you. This is your choice to make. The second document simply states you understand the terms I have laid out to you and you have accepted the check in the amount of one million dollars," Mr. Pagent said as he placed the two documents out on the coffee table for Sloanne to go over.

She studied the two documents carefully. They were both laid out in a straight-forward manner and Sloanne believed she understood them completely. She accepted the pen Mr. Pagent offered her and affixed her signature to both of the documents and then handed them back to him. She knew her life would never be the same from this moment on. Everything would change in some way and she didn't know if that would be a good thing or not. But, she resigned herself to whatever was in store and to try to do the best she could.

"I know all this is rather intimidating for you, Miss Kelly, but Mr. Miera had faith in you and I considered him an absolutely excellent judge of character. I know you will do well and I am at your service. Please don't hesitate to call me," and with that, Mr. Pagent stood and took Sloanne's offered hand.

She escorted Mr. Pagent to the front door and thanked him for everything, promising to contact him in a few days. As he headed for his limo, Sloanne saw Shawn pull in the drive and get out of his truck. She was still reeling from all the news of Mr. Miera and his estate and it must have been evident on her face.

"Okay, so what is up? You look like you just hit the lottery," Shawn kidded with her as he came up the steps and in the house.

"Actually, you could say I did."

Sloanne smiled as she began to relay the events that transpired in Chloe's living room. Mr. Pagent left copies of the two documents Sloanne signed along with a folder full of documents for her to go over. Sloanne passed Mr. Pagent's card to Shawn as she told the story. It took a few minutes to tell Shawn everything and a few more minutes for him to speak again.

"Wouldn't my momma be proud! Her son is dating an heiress. Can I get your autograph?" Shawn teased with a smile. Sloanne slapped at Shawn with a grin, but she wondered how he would feel about her now.

As if he could read her mind, he said, "Sloanne, I think you know how I feel and you should never worry about that changing."

He planted a kiss on her lips. She didn't know if it was the fact she was now rich or if it was the kiss that made her feel light-headed, but she liked it.

Just as Shawn was leaning away from her, Chloe came down the stairs with a puzzled look and asked, "What's going on? You guys look like the cats that ate the canary. Did something happen while I was asleep?"

"Ed McMahon just left, but other than that…" Shawn teased Sloanne again.

"What? Who? What's going on?" Chloe asked.

Sloanne began to tell the story yet again and they all discussed the revelation for quite awhile.

She had a lot of things to figure out in her mind. One of the most important being, did she want to continue on in interior design or would she like to do something else, like follow in her father's footsteps? She always considered doing law enforcement work, but didn't know if she was really cut-out for it. She knew she had to make some big decisions, but first she had to find out who killed Danni and try to help get Kimmi and Kammi back home. What she just learned about her future, paled in comparison to these two facts. Perhaps the answers to all her questions would lie at the end of this road.

CRUELTY TO INNOCENTS

EIGHTEEN

Havre de Grace

Four miles away in the small community of Havre de Grace, football was king and no one knew this better than Nona Carver. Nona was a petite, red-haired, single mom of two, who had high hopes for her son's career as a football player. She also intended for her daughter to excel in her education so she would never have to rely on anyone. She vigorously instilled this dream into her son's and daughter's psyche since birth. Many looked at Nona as a pushy, overbearing woman, but it made no difference to her. She was determined no child of hers would spend their whole life in a small town, with a dead-end job and no prospects. She wanted big things for them both and she set out at every turn to see they achieved her goals for them.

Nona was born and raised in Havre de Grace and followed in the path of her mother. She was the cheerleader, the Homecoming Queen and the area beauty pageant pro, but none of those things had gotten her anywhere. She married young—fresh out of high school—to the star forward of the Havre de Grace basketball team, but that marriage hadn't been good or very long and his trip to college and recruitment into semi-pro basketball had almost certainly been the end. After just six short years of marriage her husband moved on to what he referred to as 'greener pastures' and Nona was left with a small son to raise and a daughter who would be making her way into the world any day. That was the day her life changed; the day Nona made a decision to do everything in her power to ensure a good life for her children. That day, she placed a football into her son Jacob's hands and not a day passed since, that he didn't carry one around. When Nona's daughter, Hailey was born, Nona began immediately with the "Your Baby Can Read" audio books and the child had become, quite literally, a tiny genius.

Jacob Carver was a seventeen-year-old senior and star wide-receiver for the Havre de Grace high school football team. Jacob was a red-head like his mom, standing five-eleven and weighing in at one hundred ninety-five pounds. He did not look like the average wide-receiver, however he was highly sought after due to his record of one hundred thirty-one receptions as a junior and his uncanny ability to lead a team. As the new season was beginning, Jacob and his coach had high hopes that he would break the senior high school record of one hundred thirty-five receptions and lead his team to the state championships. He was at the top of the list of candidates being sought after by college football teams and not a day went by that another NCAA college coach wasn't drooling over his record or a recruiter knocking at his door or ringing his phone. Add in the fact that he could run the forty in 3.9 seconds and that he maintained a grade-point average of 3.9 and Jacob Carver was pure gold.

CRUELTY TO INNOCENTS

Hailey Carver was the spitting image of her mom except for the fact, she was intelligent enough to have been passed from fifth to seventh grade at age eleven and also to be in the Accelerated Learning Program at Havre de Grace High School.

Hailey was a very beautiful girl who carried herself with grace and poise. She would have liked to join the ranks of beauty queens in the area, but Nona would not have it. So Hailey dove deeper into her studies and was now ranked in the top two percent academically in the nation. Because of her brother's popularity at school, Hailey had been a shoe-in for the team mascot position. Having always wanted to be a beauty queen, Nona indulged her daughter in this one extra-curricular activity as a means of keeping her kids close enough where she could watchfully guide them in her role as a team chaperone.

This particular evening Nona and Hailey were in their car following along behind the team bus on their way home from the first game of the season with Joppatowne High. It had begun to rain half-way through the game and now the down-pour was making visibility difficult and driving treacherous along I-95 North. Nona was carefully negotiating the highway behind the bus while Hailey slept soundly in the back seat.

Ahead of the bus, a wrong move made by another vehicle, caused an eighteen-wheeler to lock up its brakes. Due to the rain-slicked roads, the trailer of the truck jack-knifed and turned completely sideways, blocking both right-hand lanes of traffic. The bus driver's first instinct was to slam on his brakes, which proved to be a mistake. The bus veered off the shoulder of the road which set into motion a chain of events that could not be stopped. The lean of the bus caused it to teeter and the momentum forced it further off the road. As the bus careened quickly off the asphalt and down the slope, it slammed into a concrete culvert then rolled onto its side, sliding down into a deep ravine that rimmed a large reservoir of water.

Panic gripped Nona as she watched the lights of the bus disappear into the darkness. She wheeled to the side of the highway and immediately jumped out and ran down the embankment, leaving Hailey in the back seat sleeping peacefully. Other cars were also pulling over to see the mayhem or to offer assistance to the students and mass confusion ensued.

Nona slipped on the wet grass and slid half-way down the embankment landing on the undercarriage of the toppled bus, all the while screaming her son's name at the top of her lungs. She made her way around the back of the bus to try to open the emergency exit, but it was crumpled and jammed from the impact and she was unable to budge it. Several men ran up and tried to open the exit, but to no avail.

An older gentleman appeared out of the dark carrying a huge, lug wrench. Nona yelled at the man to help with the exit door, but he was unable to hear her over the pouring rain and the screams of the boys in the bus. He proceeded straight to the front windshield of the vehicle and with one huge swing, shattered the glass and then started clearing shards from around the frame of the windshield so he could get inside without injury.

The bus was situated in such a manner, that it was listing to one side and every movement made it teeter and slip just a little further down the embankment. The sloping path the bus had taken down the embankment was now turning into a slippery wash that was piling mud against the undercarriage of the vehicle and the added weight was causing the bus to slip further down the hill. Little by little the bus was slowly moving toward the large reservoir of water at the bottom of the embankment.

The man who knocked out the window seemed to take command of the scene. He stuck his head and shoulders into the front window of the bus to check the pulse of the driver who had been thrown, head-long, into the side door of the vehicle. Not feeling any pulse, the man signaled to the other three men who were still trying to open the back exit, to come around and help him move the man out of the way. Nona and the three men quickly made their way to the front of the bus and the men helped remove the bus driver's limp body from the only exit now available to the students on the bus.

By this time, someone up on the highway had called 9-1-1

and Nona could hear the distant sirens as emergency crews raced to the scene. She became hysterical at the sight of the dead driver. Her motherly instincts took over and she lunged for the open windshield of the bus, all the while screaming her son's name.

The cool-headed gentleman grabbed Nona and shook her to get her attention.

"Ma'am! Is your son on this bus?" he asked loudly.

"Yes, my son, Jacob. Please! Jacob!"

"I need you to stay calm. Do you see that water down there? This bus is sliding towards it, so if you want to help, stand clear and let us get these boys out before they end up underwater. Any movement could send them barreling towards it. Do you understand me?" the man yelled in a commanding voice.

"Yes, I'm sorry. Please help my son," Nona begged with anguish.

The gentleman turned back to the open window of the bus and began to yell into the dark void.

"I need you boys to listen to me. You all need to be still and quiet. I need to know how many of you are hurt," yelled the old man.

"Everybody seems to be okay except Guthry. I think his leg may be broken," came the voice of Jacob Carver.

"Okay boys, this bus is sliding towards that water and you all need to move easy. One at a time, starting with those closest to this window, move toward me as carefully as you can. I'll grab each of you as you get close and help you out, but you all need to go as easy as possible," the man yelled to the boys.

Jacob was in the front of the bus and started helping each boy, one at a time, make their way to the front and out the window to the waiting men. The bus remained stable while most of the boys escaped until there were only three left on board: Jacob, Guthry—whose leg was injured—and one other team member.

As the two boys tried lifting their injured friend, the bus moaned and finally gave way to gravity, sliding down the hill rapidly and hitting the water hard with a huge splash that could be heard but not seen. The crowd gathered on the highway and the rescued boys gasped as they looked on helplessly. Nona watched her only son slip away.

The old man jumped into action and raced, blindly, towards the water falling down and sliding to a stop at the water's edge. He jumped up and dove into the water disappearing into darkness. By this time, rescue workers made their way to the scene and were rushing towards the water with lights and equipment. The old man made his way to the front of the half-submerged bus and ducked inside to try to grab the three boys. He reached Guthry first and pulled him towards the hole and out to freedom. Shoving the boy in the direction of an emergency worker who had also entered the water, the old man turned and ducked back into the quickly, sinking bus.

Nona was hysterical as she watched and waited for a sign of her son. Just then, three heads broke the surface of the water and started swimming in the direction of the shore as the crippled bus finally went under.

As the last three made their way on shore, Nona ran to her son and threw her arms around him, sobbing uncontrollably. Rescue personnel along the highway rigged up a nylon rope as a come-along that reached the waters edge. Blankets were being passed to all the boys and then each person was being tied off and pulled to safety at the top of the ravine. Guthry and the body of the bus driver were the last ones to be brought up from the dark abyss. Guthry was strapped to a gurney and being aided by two rescue workers and the old man who essentially saved all the boys' lives.

Applause rang out from the crowd and camera flashes blinded the survivors of the wreck. Guthry was rushed to a waiting ambulance while the other boys were being checked for injuries and one by one, given a clean bill of health.

Birney Sullivan ran up to Jacob Carver and asked him how he felt about being a hero.

"I'm not the hero. This man here is," Jacob replied and gestured to the old man beside him. Birney immediately turned to the man and began asking him questions while Jacob and Nona headed in the direction of their car which was still idling on the side of the highway.

As they neared their vehicle, Nona noticed the interior light was shining brightly. Jacob also noticed and asked her if she left the door open. She replayed the scene in her mind trying to recall whether or not she left the door ajar.

She turned to her son and said, "No. I was upset, of course, but I distinctly remember closing it."

Jacob threw off the blanket and ran, full speed, to the car to check on his sister. He jerked the door open and found the back seat empty except for the two red and blue pom-poms he knew belonged to her. Nona felt the sickening feeling of fear rising as she saw the look of panic spread over her son's face.

****

Could this be more perfect? There she is by the side of the highway, sleeping like an angel. All alone and waiting for me. I have to be careful. I have to blend in. It is fate that I found her here, as if she has called me to her. No one is watching as I slip silently to her side. I take her into my arms and she is mine forever.

NINETEEN

Uncovered

Sloanne, Shawn and Chloe continued to talk about the large windfall Sloanne just received. They all seemed to be in a brighter mood and Shawn had a great time kidding Sloanne about her 'new money'. It was almost like nothing bad was happening…for a few minutes.

Sloanne remembered about the forensic pictures Shawn had gone to retrieve from Patty and as much as she hated to bring them all down, she felt they needed to put their attention back on the case. The clock was ticking.

"Shawn, where are those photos?" Sloanne asked. "Have you seen them yet?"

"I've got them. Jack Parsons sent them along with a little something extra he thought Patty would want to see," Shawn replied.

"What photos?" Chloe asked.

"Chloe, I didn't know how to tell you, but we have been sent photos of Danni and the injuries she sustained. We are hoping to find something to link Danni's murder to anyone or any place in particular," said Sloanne.

A shroud of morose clouded Chloe's features and her head dropped.

"I can handle anything and I want to know everything. I want to help in every way I can. But I can never look at those photos. The last time I saw Danni, she was my beautiful, happy, little angel. I'd just rather not see anything that would change my memory. Do you understand, Sloanne?" Chloe asked quietly.

"I understand and this is not something I really want to do either. But if it will help us find out who is taking these kids and hurting them, then I have to do it," Sloanne replied.

"Okay. I think I'll go and find us all something to eat. Would you guys like some coffee?" Chloe asked trying to lighten the mood.

"That would be great. I'm starved and a little caffeine would work wonders for me," Shawn replied to Chloe.

She got up and started for the kitchen, but Sloanne grabbed her hand and asked, "Are you sure you're okay?"

"I don't know what I am, but the sooner you figure out who this guy is, the better I will be," with that, Chloe turned to head for the kitchen, but then stopped and turned back to Sloanne.

"Sloanne, I never tell you enough, how much I love you and how proud I am of you."

"I know that already. You don't have to say it."

"No, I do have to say it. And one more thing...you were meant to do this. You were always meant to follow in your dad's footsteps," Chloe gave her a half-smile—the best she could do at this point—as she left Sloanne and Shawn alone.

Sloanne smiled at the honesty of her words, as if Chloe read her thoughts. Maybe she really was meant to do this kind of work. She thought about it many times, but having gone through all this with Chloe and Danni made her see that, not only was there a need for her in law enforcement, she loved the work. This was a hard world and bad things did happen to good people. She never wanted to see people suffer. Her dad had been like that. He believed in justice and in fairness. For the first time in her life, she knew the best way to honor him and herself, was to be like him. To try to make a difference and ease some of the suffering in the world. She would start now, by throwing herself into the task of catching a killer...Danni's killer.

"Earth to Sloanne...Hello!"

Shawn snapped his fingers trying to bring Sloanne back to the here and now. Once she realized what he was doing, she could not help but laugh at him and herself. She stuck her hand out with her index finger pointing at him. He looked at her with an inquisitive expression and she brought her finger up and flicked his nose quickly and then laughed at the surprised look on his face. He laughed at her little trick as he grabbed the envelope that contained the forensic photos and the report from Jack and handed it to her. She looked at the envelope with dread, but quickly opened it and removed the contents.

The envelope contained several photos of various parts of Danni's body and the report. Sloanne closed her eyes and unconsciously held her breath as she laid them all out on the coffee table. Shawn's eyes swept over the photos and he made an agonized groan in his throat. They both hesitated, but then Shawn laid his hand on Sloanne's to reassure her. Three of the photos were of Danni's wrists and a strangely-shaped bruised area. Sloanne wondered what could have made marks like that and as she raised her eyes to Shawn, he started reading aloud the report that Jack enclosed.

I have enclosed the photos and the coroner's findings, as per your request. I know that you will find the markings on the victim's wrists and ankles unusual, as I did. I did a little research and uncovered some information that you may find useful.

Sloanne picked up the two photos of Danni's ankles and looked at them closely while Shawn continued to read.

The markings are specific to a particular model of bondage equipment. This device is not widely available and can only be purchased through illegal black-market sources. The manufacturer discontinued production of this item when a child pornography case in Germany was linked to the use of this particular restraint. I have enclosed a web link to the site which includes information on the two and a half year long investigation of a child-pornography ring and their tie-in with this device. The site will give you information on the device, how it is used and also some information on other porn sites involving children. This seems to be an on-going investigation and it's not limited to one country, but involves several others besides Germany, including the US.

Of course, you know this information is on a 'need-to-know' basis. If you need anything else, please feel free to contact me at my office.

Sincerely,

Jack Parsons, Chief of Forensics

Harford County, Bel Air, MD

"So, obviously Jack thinks Danni's death had something to do with kiddy porn," Sloanne commented.

"That would be my guess. My god, how can anyone do such awful shit to another human being, especially a kid?" Shawn breathed with disgust.

"Hundreds of child-pornography rings are uncovered every year in the US alone. To say nothing about the ones that are never exposed. Imagine the number of pedophiles in the world and in each one, you have the potential for a child to be abused. There could literally be millions out there doing things they will never get caught doing. World-wide it's a freaking epidemic. Everyday children are being taken and then sold into sexual-slavery all over the world," Sloanne stated.

"Damn. I knew there were some sick people out there, but I had no idea how bad it was," Shawn was incredulous.

"Many people don't. It's just easier for people to live in

oblivion until, of course, it happens to their family or someone they know. If they pretend it doesn't exist then maybe it won't," replied Sloanne.

"I can't stomach the thought of my nieces out there all alone and scared, being tortured or worse," Shawn said with emotion.

Sloanne detected a hitch in his voice and she realized he did not want to show this side of himself to her. He was trying to be strong for her and for his family.

"How many kids do they usually find, Sloanne? I mean, is there still a chance we can get the girls back?" he asked in a pleading voice.

"The statistics get worse and worse with every hour that slips by. The more time that passes, the lower our chances are of ever finding those girls again. We won't give up, Shawn. I will not stop until we find the girls and bring them home, I promise. This maniac must be stopped or he'll keep on taking children. That is what he does. He will never stop and we can't either," she said with conviction.

"I think we should search the Internet and see if we can find any other sites that look like they could be linked to our case. We'll start with the links Jack gave Patty and work from there," Sloanne said as she stood to retrieve the laptop case she left in Shawn's truck.

She headed for the front door and out to the drive with Shawn right behind her. He unlocked the truck door and opened it so

Sloanne could reach in and grab the case. Just as she backed out of the truck, she heard the sound of a car passing.

"Look who's riding by to check on our well-being. Skippy must be on the 'neighborhood watch'," Shawn said sarcastically as he threw up his hand in a wave that turned into a middle-finger salute.

Sloanne looked up to see Skip riding by in his very-shiny Porsche. Skip was watching them as they stood by Shawn's truck. As Shawn gave him the finger, he gunned the engine and peeled away down the street.

"Guess the ol' boy didn't dig my greeting," Shawn said with that big grin of his.

"Okay! Clearly Skip is watching us. First, he drove by your place and he's driven by here more than once. He even drove by my parents' house while we were there. What the hell is he looking for? I find it hard to believe all this is about me. He has women crawling out of the woodwork. What's the attraction with us? Something just is not right with him. Look at that car. Does that ring any bells with you? He has a reputation of roughing up young girls and we already know he has a taste for S&M. Do you think it is possible that Skip could be involved in all this in some way?" Sloanne asked now, voicing her private suspicions for the first time.

"Come on, Sloanne. I know the guy's a creep, but is he really capable of what we're talking about here? I mean, you used to date the guy, right? Do you think he is sick enough to do what was done to Danni?"

"We dated yes, but that was a lifetime ago. I'm telling you, Skip has changed and not for the better. The other night at the restaurant, there was something in his eyes I've never seen before. Something about him was all wrong. I was really frightened of what he might be capable of. Now, I'm thinking he's more than capable of what we're talking about. Do you remember saying something about Skip having a place in Rock Hall? He said something to me about it too. Do you know where this place is?"

"No, Sloanne, but I bet it wouldn't be hard to find out were it is. We could always check land records, couldn't we?"

"You're right. Someone who has something to hide would need a private place to hide it. Rock Hall is a pretty secluded area. It would be a perfect place to hide little girls."

Sloanne and Shawn walked back to the house and Sloanne set up the computer. They begin with the site Jack Parsons suggested which led to more sites. It was hard to believe how many websites were based on kiddy porn.

Chloe came in with a large tray of food and coffee and Shawn immediately began to grab up the photos and the report they had spread out on the coffee table and shove them back into the file folder. Chloe stood holding the tray for a moment and then said, "I know you guys want to protect me, but I need to be doing something to help. I don't know if I'm ready, but I can't sit by and do nothing. I need to be a part of this for myself and for Danni."

Sloanne looked into the eyes of her friend and then patted the seat beside her for Chloe to sit. The three of them began to eat in silence.

It got later and later in the evening and they were still hard at it. They worked through the rest of the night looking through the Internet and going over some of the evidence they amassed. Sloanne made several calls to Patty, but only reached his voicemail. She felt confident he would show up or call at any minute and then he would be able to shed some light on the files they dug up at her parent's home.

The time easily slipped away from them as they toiled for hours in search of any clue that could lead them to the missing girls and inevitably to Danni's killer. The storm that had blown up went virtually unnoticed by the three as they worked.

At one point, as they again went through the newspaper articles, Chloe found a particular photo that seemed to hold her attention. Sloanne noticed the intent way she was studying the photo as she tilted it this way and that.

"Sloanne, what does this look like to you?" Chloe asked pointing to a wide-angle shot of the house fire where Kimmi and Kammi had been taken.

Sloanne took the photo from Chloe. The photo was that of

the crowd gathered in the street as the firemen battled the blaze. Several police cars and fire trucks were visible, as was the Tyler's mini-van. In the back seat, plainly in view, were the faces of Kimmi and Kammi Tyler. There seemed to be a lot of action going on and people standing around, but Sloanne detected nothing out of the ordinary.

"What are you seeing that I'm not, Chloe?"

"There…right there! That light or flash. What is that?" Chloe pointed to a small dark area with a single bright spot. "Is that a flash from a camera?"

"I don't know. Doesn't look like much. Maybe just a reflection off something." she replied.

"Let me see," Shawn said. He took the photo from Sloanne and studied it for a moment and then said, "If Kimmi and Kammi are still in the car in this photo, wouldn't that mean one of the people standing around might have been the kidnapper or at least seen the kidnapper whether they knew it or not?"

"The police have questioned everyone in this photo and they all check out," Sloanne replied.

"If I didn't know any better, I'd be willing to think Birney Sullivan is the kidnapper. I mean, he's been at every scene and was always around when these kids were being taken," Chloe said hesitantly.

"Evidently, the police thought of him too. He has been

238

checked out and questioned. The police must have been satisfied with what he had to say because they aren't even considering him at this point." Sloanne said.

Just as Sloanne finished her comment, her cell rang shrilly, startling them all. She grabbed it up and saw it was Patty and felt relieved he was finally calling.

"Hey, kiddo, what's up? You guys still awake?" Patty's warm voice filled Sloanne's ear.

"Hey, where the heck have you been? I have called several times and I was starting to worry," Sloanne breathed into the phone.

"Detective Howard and I have been following a few leads and we were out of signal range. Sorry about that, but you know better than to worry about me. What's this about some old case files of your dad's?" Patty asked.

"We found some case files Dad saved in the attic. It is a case you and he worked on about twenty-five years ago that involved some kidnappings which seem similar to ours. I really wanted you to look through them and tell me what you remember about it. Can you come by now?" Sloanne explained to Patty.

"Oh, kiddo! I don't think my mind could process anything else tonight. I've been going for twenty-four hours straight. Could we do this first thing in the morning?" he asked.

"Okay. I know you are tired. Get a few hours sleep and call me the minute you get up. I think your input could really be helpful and I'm anxious to pick your brain."

"You know, you are getting pretty good at this detective stuff, kiddo. But then you always were your daddy's girl."

"I will take that as a compliment. I love you, Patty. Sleep well."

"Love you too, kiddo. Goodnight."

It had gotten really late. Chloe had given up an hour earlier and gone to bed. Shawn stretched out on the sofa for just a minute and of course, fell quietly asleep. As he snored softly, Sloanne was still going at it. She went through what seemed like a thousand websites. Some of the images were enough to make her almost physically ill, but she knew she had to see them and she continued to study them. At one point, on a particularly sleazy site, Sloanne found hundreds of pictures of young or adolescent girls posed on strange-looking, restraint devices in all manner of sexual poses. She could hardly stand to look at them, but she could not take her eyes away. She knew there were sick people out there, but even she could not believe what she was seeing.

Photo after photo burned into Sloanne's mind. She tasted the bile rising in the back of her throat and swallowed hard to keep it at bay. Each girl in the photos seemed younger than the last and Sloanne squeezed her eyes tightly shut to push back the dizziness that crept up on her. When she felt she could not take another second of looking through the photos, one jumped out at her.

The young girl looked so familiar to her, but what caught her eye was the machine the girl was posed on. It resembled the one Jack Parsons referred to and from what Sloanne could see, the wrist and ankle restraints looked as if they could leave the same tale-tell marks as the ones on Danni.

The angle of the photo Sloanne was seeing was only an extreme profile. The girl's face was almost completely away from Sloanne except for a small portion of the side of her face. But the more Sloanne looked at the image, the more she was convinced, she was looking at a picture of Danni's last hours. There was no way for Sloanne to be sure that this photo was actually Danni. It would never pass any identification test, but in her mind and gut...this was Danni!

This image was one Sloanne would never be able to shake. She knew she would never knowingly allow anyone to see the image even though millions of sick people probably already had.

She was drained now and laid down next to Shawn as he slept on the sofa. She was so tired, but her mind kept racing and going back to the images of the maybe-Danni. She didn't really want to sleep, but she was so exhausted her eyes were blurry. She felt herself floating and she thought she heard Danni whisper, "You're almost there."

****

WHAM!!! Shawn and Sloanne nearly fell off the couch at the

loud smack on the coffee table in front of them. There stood Chloe with her hand on the morning paper looking smugly at them both.

"I told you it was something...look at this. How can the same 'nothing' be in two different pictures?" Chloe asked urgently.

Sloanne and Shawn were so surprised by Chloe's outburst and the fact they had been jolted from their sleep, they were both speechless.

"Another kid was taken last night and look at this," she said handing the paper to Sloanne.

The front page headlines screamed, *FOURTH CHILD ABDUCTED FROM 911 EMERGENCY SCENE*! Sloanne nearly dropped the paper. The picture under the caption depicted a large crowd of onlookers at the side of a highway looking partially down a ravine and there in the dark periphery was what appeared to be an over-turned, half-submerged school bus. Students were being hauled up on a rope and there was even a gurney with someone strapped to it surrounded by two EMTs. The picture was taken at an angle so part of it showed a line of cars and a section of the highway.

As Sloanne looked closer, she saw what Chloe was seeing. There, in a small dark area of the photo, was what looked like a small flash of light just like in the other news image. Shawn saw it about a second after Sloanne.

"I'll be damned. Look at that. What the hell is that?" Shawn asked.

"I don't know what it is, but it isn't a reflection. The angle is wrong and I don't see anything that could cause that. Chloe, you just may have found something," Sloanne beamed at her friend.

"Well, I know how hard it is for you two to find these clues and I know you need me to lead you sometime, but don't count on it happening again. And by the way, please notice the bi-line, another great image by none other than our resident reporter, Mr. Snake-in-a-Suit, Birney Sullivan. Don't you think you two should maybe go see this guy or do I have to do everything," Chloe tittered with an elevated air.

"I guess we should go see the snake then," Shawn said sarcastically.

"I think we should go see him," Sloanne said in a silly voice.

The three laughed at the conversation and then Shawn and Sloanne got up and gathered the photos to take to Sullivan's office. They intended to find out what the strange flash was and Sloanne hoped Patty had been right when he said Birney was a good guy. Mr. Snake could have the key that would help them unravel this case.

TWENTY

Birney

Chloe and Sloanne made off in different directions. Chloe towards the kitchen to make lunch and coffee and Sloanne went to her room at the top of the stairs to get showered and changed.

Shawn found himself alone, sitting in the living room with time to think over everything that transpired during the past two weeks. He reminisced over his and Sloanne's first meeting at the scene of the wreck and he remembered their days together in high school. Sloanne had been a beautiful girl then, of course, but that paled in comparison to how stunning she was now. He was amazed at how far she had come in her life and how intelligent she was. He never suspected the girl he'd known in school would turn out to be the woman she was now. Shawn smiled to himself as he thought of his mother and father and how they would have adored a girl like Sloanne. He was unsure of what their future held, but he knew without question, Sloanne had become a huge part of his life in a very short time. He was determined she would share his life for the long-term and he hoped she felt the same about him. He had to admit to himself he was falling in love with her.

Chloe peeked around the corner to say something to Shawn, but noticed he was deep in thought, so she decided to wait to talk with him. Just as she turned back to the kitchen, Sloanne came down the stairs looking refreshed and ready for the trip to Birney's.

The group quickly ate and just as they were finishing, Chloe spoke up.

"Guys, this is where I bow out. I think I need to get myself together. You two are doing a fantastic job and I appreciate everything, but I have to get things in order here and think about going back to work. I miss Danni terribly, but the only way for me to make it through, is to put everything in my life back in order. Danni would have wanted it that way," Chloe said, softly to Sloanne and Shawn.

"I know how you feel, Chloe and I understand. I miss Danni too. I want your life to be as normal as possible from here on out. If you think you're better off doing your own thing here, then I am all for that. Shawn and I will keep you informed about what is going on and you can do what you need to do."   Sloanne bent to hug her best friend.

"I'm so glad you guys understand. Now get out there and do what you do best. Those three little girls are waiting for you. You need to hurry and find this psycho before he kills another child. I love you guys and if you need me, just call. Be careful and I'll see you guys later."

With that, Chloe turned and went up the stairs.

Sloanne grabbed the folder containing the pictures they wanted to discuss with Birney and her laptop case while Shawn grabbed his keys. They headed out the door and jumped in Shawn's truck. He wanted to stop by his place and take a quick shower and Sloanne thought it would be the perfect opportunity for her to do a little more Internet sleuthing and give Patty a call. She had nearly forgotten he was coming over to Chloe's and she wanted to head him off and arrange a time they could get together.

While Shawn took a shower and dressed, Sloanne looked through a few sites. She also made a quick call to Patty, but his phone went straight to voicemail. Sloanne left him a message to call her later to discuss the files they found and to let him know about the lead they discovered in the news photos. She also told him they were heading to Birney's. Just as Sloanne hung up, Shawn's voice came from behind her.

"Are you ready to go?"

They left Shawn's apartment and as they did, Skip Perryman's unmistakable vehicle could be seen parked a few houses down the street. Shawn held back his gut instinct to walk over, drag Skip from his car and punch him. Instead, he calmly asked Sloanne for her cell phone. He dialed a number and began to speak.

"Chief Williams, please," Shawn said into the phone as Sloanne stood by with a puzzled look.

"Yes sir, this is Shawn Tyler from the fire department. I'm good, sir. How are you? Listen, I was calling to report a suspicious vehicle in my neighborhood. You know where I live, don't you, sir?

Good. The vehicle is a dark-colored sports car with a white male sitting inside. With all the trouble we're having in Aberdeen, I thought you might want to know about something like this. I believe I've seen this same car in the area before and I'm beginning to wonder why. Yes, sir. You're very welcome. Always glad to help the local police curb the crime rate. You take care now. Thank you," Shawn closed Sloanne's cell phone and handed it back to her.

The smile on Sloanne's face was contagious and now they were both grinning at Shawn's little pay-back to Skip.

The two got into Shawn's truck and waited. Within two minutes of the call, three police cruisers came barreling down Shawn's street, one from the east and two from the west. Before Skip could even process what was happening, the three cars surrounded his vehicle and boxed him in. Shawn almost hurt himself laughing and Sloanne could not help but laugh with him.

"I guess that will keep ol' Skip busy for awhile," Shawn said with an obvious grin.

"That should definitely get us out of here without being followed anyway," Sloanne replied back.

Shawn eased his truck into the road and passed by the situation unfolding at Skip's car. As they did, Shawn turned and smiled at Skip and gave him a grin and a nice little salute. Shawn gunned his truck and the pair headed in the direction of the newspaper office where Birney Sullivan worked.

Sloanne called the newspaper office to make sure Birney was in. She was told he just left to go home for lunch and the lady proceeded to give Sloanne his address in a small apartment complex down from the news office.

Shawn pulled his truck into an empty parking spot in Birney's complex and he and Sloanne jumped out and headed to Birney's front door. Just as Sloanne raised her hand to knock, Birney swung open the door and motioned them in.

"Madge at the office called and said you were heading over, Sloanne. I'm glad you came by. I knew your dad and I had the utmost respect for him. He was a great detective and an asset to police work. Now, what can I help you with?" Birney asked with a smile.

Sloanne was taken aback at the welcoming demeanor of Birney. Patty had been right when he said Birney was a good guy. She was feeling more and more confident they were on to something and had been right in coming here.

Sloanne and Shawn entered Birney's house and he motioned for them to sit down in the front room.

"Can I get you two anything? I don't get many visitors," Birney said.

"No thanks, Birney. We just wanted to ask you a few questions about the photos you've taken at the kidnapping scenes," Sloanne said.

248

"Well, I've told the police everything I can think of, but I wasn't much help," replied Birney.

"What about this," Sloanne said pointing to one of the photos she brought.

Birney took the photo from Sloanne to get a better look at what she was pointing to. He looked closely at the photo, dropping down the glasses perched on his head and picked up a small magnifying glass lying on his coffee table. He then looked at the photo again, studying it intently.

"This isn't very clear. Doesn't really look like anything much to me," Birney said.

"Okay, what about this?" Sloanne said pointing to another photo she produced from the folder in her lap.

Birney took the next photo and held the two side-by-side.

"Well, looks like the same thing on both pictures, but it's a little grainy. I think I've got the originals of these photos in my files. Let me go get them and we can get a better look. I'll be right back."

Birney headed towards the back of the apartment to another room as Sloanne and Shawn waited.

A few moments passed and as Birney walked back into the living room, he was studying both pictures, but these were originals and much clearer.

"Well, I've been taking photos a long time and I know that certain types of light give off distinct patterns on film. This one is unmistakable," he said

"What is it?" Sloanne asked anxiously.

"Simple. I believe it is the flash from a cigarette lighter. Looks like someone is striking the flint, but not actually lighting the flame. I would guess a Zippo. Disposable lighters don't really work like that," Birney replied to Sloanne.

"So you're saying that someone is standing at a distance from where you were shooting and flicking a lighter?" Shawn asked.

"That's exactly what I'm saying and this is a pretty good clue you two have found. Don't know how I missed that. Must be getting old," Birney said.

"This is great, Birney. You don't know how much you have helped. I am glad to know we could count on you and I hope you won't mind if we need your help again in the future," Sloanne said sweetly to the man.

Birney blushed and grinned at Sloanne.

"Anything for the lovely daughter of Erin Kelly. But you guys don't have to rush off do you?" Birney asked Sloanne, who was now rising from her seat.

She was so excited by what she just heard and she wanted to get Shawn out of there and back to the truck so she could talk to him in private. She grabbed his hand and nearly jerked him to his feet. He came up with a startled look on his face and Sloanne began pulling him in the direction of Birney's front door.

"We really have to go. We have another lead to follow and the clock is ticking. You have been so helpful Birney. We really appreciate your time."

With that Sloanne leaned in and planted a peck on Birney's cheek. The man got visible giddy and could only grin as Sloanne and Shawn hurried out the front door and back to the truck.

TWENTY-ONE

Suspicious

Once they were both seated in the truck, Sloanne immediately turned to Shawn.

"There was something that I didn't mention about that night at the restaurant with Skip," Sloanne said anxiously.

"What? Did that creep try something?" Shawn asked with a touch of anger.

"No, Shawn, nothing like that. Just something I noticed he kept doing and at the time, dismissed as a nervous tick."

"Okay, what?"

"Skip kept opening and closing a gold Zippo lighter. It was strange. He would open it, strike the flint, but not light the flame and then close it all in one swift movement. I'm certain he was not even aware he was doing it. I remember because it was annoying as hell and just not something you see people doing."

"Son-of-a-bitch! I'll kill him!" Shawn vehemently spat through gritted teeth.

"No, you won't. We will do this the right way, or not at all. Please, Shawn, can I count on you to keep it together?"

"Yes, yes, yes, but can I punch the bastard when we catch him?"

"*If* we catch him. We don't have enough proof yet, Shawn.

But we are close. I can feel it."

As Sloanne uttered the words the faint whisper of Danni's voice drifted into her mind, '*you're almost there*'.

"Where to now, Detective Kelly?" Shawn asked next.

"City Hall, we have to find out if there are any properties in Rock Hall that are registered in Skip Perryman's name."

"You got it. You may want to put your seatbelt on," Shawn said.

And with that he gunned the truck and headed for the courthouse.

As they rode, Sloanne's cell began to ring.

"Hello."

"Hey, Sloanne, this is Howard. Listen, I just wanted to let you know the Williams girl is waking up and trying to talk. We're hoping she can ID our perp, but she's not all the way out of it and we have to wait for her doctor. This could be the break we've been looking for. Patty told me that you are doing some investigating on your own. I don't have a problem with that, but my Captain surely would. Please don't do anything stupid or heroic. Call me if you run across anything I can use."

"That's great, Howard. Shawn and I are following up on a few leads of our own and we may have found something, but we're not sure just yet. Please keep us posted on Simone and we will let you know if our leads pan out."

"You got it, Sloanne. By the way, have you seen Patty today?"

"I have not talked to him, but I did leave him a voice mail earlier."

"I've left him a few myself. If you talk to him before I do, let him know I'm looking for him and ask him to call me ASAP. I'd appreciate it, Sloanne."

"I'll certainly do it, Howard. Talk to you soon."

Sloanne closed her cell just as Shawn pulled his truck into a parking spot in front of the courthouse and checked his watch.

"Thirty minutes until this place closes. You better hurry. I'm going to stay here and do a little more searching on the Internet. I want to see if I can dig up anything we may have missed," Shawn said, looking at Sloanne. He leaned over and placed a kiss on Sloanne's lips and then said, "Good luck, Detective."

She blushed as she jumped out of the truck and ran into the building.

Sloanne quickly located the land records office and explained to the bored-looking clerk she was searching for a piece of property in the Rock Hall area that belonged to Skip Perryman. She hated to use his name, but they were so close now and she was certain Skip was involved. The clerk motioned Sloanne around the desk to a corner with an ancient looking micro-fiche machine and a couple rows of numbered and alphabetical drawer files. The clerk explained to Sloanne, the process of finding what she needed and then turned and left. Sloanne began to go through the films looking for the records she sought.

First, Sloanne searched out all properties owned by Skylar Perryman and came up empty. As she thought about it, something dawned on Sloanne and she made a search for all properties owned by the Perryman's.

Once Sloanne weeded through the many properties owned by John, she found listings held by Rochelle and also some listed as being owned by Perryman Realty. Rochelle's real estate business owned four properties in the Rock Hall area. Two were residential and Sloanne wrote down the addresses, but they both were in busy areas. Sloanne guessed that the property she was looking for had to be secluded so she kept searching.

The next property listed was a restaurant located on the coast. Sloanne found the last property listed was an old lighthouse and keeper's dwelling on a secluded part of Harbor Highway. This sounded perfect and Sloanne figured it could be an excellent place to hide. Skip could have gotten use of the place from his mother.

Sloanne pulled out her cell phone and quickly dialed information for a listing on Perryman Realty. She got the number and dialed it, waiting as it rang.

"Perryman Realty. How may I help you?" came the voice at the other end.

"Yes, I was looking for a secluded property in the Rock Hall area and came across your listing. I was wondering if you could give me the address and directions to the place." Sloanne said nervously.

"Oh yes ma'am. You must be referring to the old lighthouse property. We have had that property for quite some time. It's a good distance from town and I guess people aren't interested in lighthouses anymore. The address is 14385 Harbor Highway. Would you like to make an appointment to look at the property?" the receptionist asked politely, but was met with nothing but silence on the other end.

Sloanne slammed her cell phone closed and raced down the courthouse steps to Shawn's truck. She was shaking with anticipation and couldn't wait to tell Shawn what she found.

"I think we've got him, Shawn. My god, here's the address to the property. That bastard and his reign of terror are coming to an end."

Shawn read the address aloud and wasted no time pulling the truck out into traffic, heading in the direction of Rock Hall.

Sloanne pulled out her cell and dialed Patty's number. She wanted to let him know what transpired and she felt he needed to be their back-up in case Skip was at the property when they arrived. The sun was slipping low and Sloanne knew it would be dark well before they got to Rock Hall.

The phone rang once and Patty answered, "Hey, kiddo,

where are you? I've been looking everywhere for you."

"Listen, Patty. We are heading for Rock Hall. We think we've found evidence that Skip Perryman is our man. His mother owns some property in Rock Hall, very secluded. It would be the perfect place to hide children. Skip has a history of being sexually dysfunctional and we believe we've found a clue that points directly at him. Trust me on this, Patty. I really believe Skip is the one who is taking these children and if he is, those girls are at this property. I know I'm right about this. I think you should call in some back-up and meet us there. The address is 14385 Harbor Highway. We don't know what we are going to find when we get there. Skip has been following us around for days so he's suspicious. He is obviously crazy and he may try anything at this point."

"Sloanne, are you sure it's Skip?"

"Yes, damn it, I'm sure."

"I'm just shocked by all this. Listen, Sloanne, you have to promise me you'll be careful. If Skip really is our man, he will not hesitate to do you or Shawn harm. He may even have a gun. If you get there and anything looks even remotely dangerous, get the hell out of there. Do you understand me?"

"Yes, Patty, but we are hoping he won't even be there. Best case, we get the kids and get out. The police can handle it from there. Just please hurry. I love you, Patty"

"I'm right behind you, kiddo and I'll be bringing the cavalry with me. I love you too, Sloanne. And I'm proud of you."

Before Sloanne could pocket her phone, it rang once again.

"Hello, Patty?" Sloanne breathed into the cell phone, thinking Patty had forgotten to tell her something.

"No, Sloanne, its Birney. Something really weird just happened. I'm sorry to say I may have given you and Shawn away."

"What do you mean, Birney? Gave us away to whom?" Sloanne asked.

"To Skip Perryman. He was just here. Raging he was and screaming at me to tell him why you two were here. He hit me over the head with a gun, Sloanne. Left a fairly nice sized goose-egg on my head. I was afraid he was going to kill me. He kept ranting about you and your boyfriend being too nosey and finding him out. I had to tell him what you wanted here. I'm sorry, Sloanne, but he was crazy. Like no one I've ever seen before. Once I told him what you two wanted, he snatched up the pictures and hauled ass out of here mumbling something about getting back at you and fixing your little boyfriend. I think he means to cause you two *a lot* of trouble."

"Birney, I'm so sorry. Are you okay? I don't blame you for telling him what you know. We are pretty sure Skip is the person who is taking the kids and he may have killed Danni too. We are headed to Rock Hall. We think he has a hideout there and that the kids may be there."

"You're kidding? Why would Skip do something like that?

He never seemed like the type for murder. I know he's had some run-ins with the law, but he's a rich kid. What would cause him to do something like this?"

"I don't know, Birney and I don't care. All I know is there are three, scared little girls out there who are waiting for someone to save them. I couldn't save Danni, but I'll be damned if I'm not going to do everything possible to save *them*."

"Do you have any idea how proud your father would be of you, Sloanne? Please be careful. Skip is a madman and he was very pissed. I think he wants you and Shawn dead. Promise me you two will be careful."

"Thanks, Birney. We will be as careful as possible. You take care of yourself now, okay? Oh, and Birney, keep that camera ready. This just may be the story of a lifetime."

Sloanne hung up the phone just as Shawn passed the road sign leaving Aberdeen. She decided she should call Chloe to let her know what they found. She understood why Chloe could not be there, but she promised to keep her informed and she intended to do just that.

Just as her hand flipped the cell open, Shawn said, "I think we should call Chloe. She should know what's happening in case something goes wrong. She needs to be aware and prepared," Shawn said in a clear, quiet voice.

"I was just about to call her. I guess great minds really do thing alike. Do you really suspect something is going to go wrong, Shawn?" Sloanne began to realize how dangerous Skip might be now that he knew they were on to him. She was starting to feel the fear creep up her spine. What if something bad did happen? What if someone got injured or killed? What if the kids were already gone? Sloanne's mind raced over the possibilities and she began to shake from adrenaline.

"Skip knows we know. He'll be desperate now. He could threaten anyone. I'm not anticipating anything bad, but we're dealing with a psycho." He then asked. "Are you afraid?"

"Heck, Mr. Big, Strong Fireman! I'm not afraid of anything when I'm with you," she said teasing Shawn, not wanting him to know how scared she really was.

She had been sitting there with her cell in her hand the entire time they were talking and finally she dialed Chloe's number. When she answered, Sloanne quickly filled her in on what was happening and the whole story behind the light in the picture. When she told her about the call from Detective Howard and about Simone Williams, Chloe said she would run up to the hospital and check on the progress of the girl. Sloanne asked her to call if Simone's condition improved and she promised she would. She asked Sloanne several times to be careful and not to do anything foolish. Sloanne promised she would be careful, told Chloe she loved her and hung up the phone. Sloanne quietly thought how glad she was that her friend was leaving her home and going to the hospital. She figured Chloe would be safe there in case Skip got any ideas about retribution.

The ride to Rock Hall took about thirty minutes, but to Shawn, it felt like an eternity. Sloanne noticed the way Shawn gripped the steering wheel as he drove and how his knuckles kept going white from the tightness of his grip. She saw the muscles of his jaw line flex and relax as he gritted his teeth in anguish. She knew he was anxious to find the girls and even more anxious to know what condition they were in. She hoped he could keep it together if they should stumble upon the worst.

Shawn's mind was in turmoil. His heart rate was through the roof and adrenaline was making sweat pour from his body. He tried to keep the speed of the truck at the posted limit, but his foot pressed harder on the accelerator. His nieces were out there and he knew he could not bare it if anything happened to them. He also knew his brother and sister-in-law would never recover if their children were not saved. Two young faces burned into his mind, but one name brought him to madness. Skip!

As they entered Rock Hall and headed in the direction of the address the receptionist gave them, Sloanne realized how easily someone could hide here. The town had always been small, but at one time, it was a thriving fishing community. Now it was little more than a few fishermen's homes, one restaurant and a run-down gas station. The entire town gave her the feeling of driving into an episode of 'The Twilight Zone'.

Harbor Highway was a winding, two-lane road that rarely caught sight of the water. It was completely lined on either side, by enormous Northern Pines and Cedars, which seemed to swallow up the road. There were no houses on the left-hand side and the only sign they saw was a realtor's sign with 'Perryman Realty' emblazoned on both sides.

"This must be it, but it just looks like an old, grown-up dirt road," Shawn said.

"Exactly! It's a perfect place to hide," Sloanne replied.

Shawn guided the truck carefully onto the dirt drive and stopped.

Turning to Sloanne he said, "This could get dangerous. Promise me, if anything happens, you will get out and find Patty. I couldn't bare it if something happened to you. Don't be stupid. Use your head. You know I care about you."

"I promise, but let's just hope nothing does go wrong. And please, don't try to be a hero, okay," Sloanne said to him.

He gave her that big grin and they started down the long, overgrown road.

They traveled along the dirt drive at least a mile before they saw the top of the lighthouse reveal itself over the dark, tree line. They looked at each other and then Shawn grabbed Sloanne's hand and gave it a simple squeeze.

They could see the clearing ahead and Shawn killed the lights and the engine and they coasted onto the edge of the property. They could see the old lighthouse and keeper's dwelling now. Sloanne could tell it had once been nice, but years of weathering the elements and much neglect, left it sagging and run-down. The lighthouse stood about twenty yards to the left of the house, its entrance partially boarded and padlocked with a sign that read 'Condemned'. The house was a small dwelling partially built of the very stone Rock Hall was famous for. All but the front door had been boarded up as if the last occupant was preparing for a huge storm. There were fresh tire treads in the drive leading to the house and a small light was visible through the breaks in the wood of the front door. No other trace of a vehicle or person could be seen. The silence and the darkness enveloped them.

Shawn reach behind the seat of his truck and pulled out a formidable looking fireman's ax; the kind that was used to smash out windows and break down doors.

Shawn could see the distress on Sloanne's face so he simply said, "Just in case…" and gave her his signature smile.

He then reached up and flipped the switch on the dome light of his truck so, when the doors were opened, the light would remain off. They both opened their doors and stepped out into the darkness, quietly re-closing them.

They walked to the front of the truck and scanned the

property one last time. Sloanne began walking towards the house. Shawn quickly stepped ahead of her, gently placing his arm in front of her and guided her carefully, a few steps behind him. He wanted her to have enough room to get away if something bad should happen. In his heart, he wanted to protect her. He wanted her as far away from here as possible, but since he knew that was out of the question, the best he could hope for was having Sloanne behind him, allowing him to first see what they were walking into.

The two cautiously made their way to the front door and Shawn turned the knob. The front door released easily and opened into a dimly lit room. The room was sparsely furnished. An old, grandfather clock stood in one corner. There were a couple of chairs, a small love seat and a television set positioned atop an antique dresser.

The room itself was littered with empty bottles of what had been expensive wine and an ashtray on the arm of the love seat overflowed with the butts of imported cigarettes. Sloanne knew right away they found Skip's hiding place and she prayed silently to herself, they would find the girls here.

Shawn stepped lightly through the room trying to keep from making any unnecessary noise. He made his way through the living room and towards a small hallway leading to the back of the house. About halfway down the hall, he came upon a door he believed led to a cellar. Shawn noticed a piece of paper lying on the floor which appeared out of place in the empty house, so he reached down to pick it up.

Sloanne saw Shawn standing in the hallway and made her way towards him. As she did, she saw him reach down and pluck something from the floor. As Shawn flipped the paper over to read it, fear and adrenaline seized him. The paper was a simple child's coloring of an angel with one word written at the top…Kimmi!

Shawn turned to Sloanne and then back to the door. Before he could think, he jerked the door open and yelled down into the darkness, "Kimmi, Kammi, are you there? It's Uncle Shawn. Are you there?"

Sloanne's eyes filled with tears as a single, small voice cried out from the abyss, "Uncle Shawn, we're here!"

TWENTY-TWO

Witness

Chloe dressed quickly and headed to the hospital. She was unsure if she would be allowed to speak with Simone Williams, but she was determined to try.

Aberdeen Memorial was just a few miles from Chloe's home and situated right in the center of a nice residential neighborhood. It had recently undergone some expansions and now was the largest medical facility in the tri-county area. It housed one of the best oncology centers in Maryland and was equipped to handle any major, medical emergency.

The entire front entrance to the facility was completely covered in smoked glass windows and two large, automatic sliding doors welcomed visitors at the front entrance.

Chloe parked her car and walked up to the massive structure, going over and over in her mind, what she would say to Simone if she were allowed to see the girl.

The doors slid quietly open and Chloe went through. She walked across the lobby stepping to a desk where several women sat engrossed in their individual tasks.

"May I help you," asked an older woman from behind the desk.

"Yes, my name is Chloe Jacobs. I'm here to see Simone

Williams. Could you tell me what room she is in, please?" replied Chloe.

The receptionist gave Chloe a puzzled look and then asked, "Are you family?"

"No, ma'am…I'm just a friend," Chloe said softly.

"Could you wait a moment?" the receptionist asked as she picked up the phone and pressed a button.

The woman began to speak softly to someone on the other end. When she finished, she instructed Chloe someone would be there to talk to her in a few minutes.

Chloe seated herself in a chair in the waiting area next to the elevators. Within a few minutes, the elevator doors opened and out stepped Detective Howard followed closely by two uniformed officers. Detective Howard saw Chloe immediately and walked to her waving off the two officers.

"Hello, Ms. Jacobs. How are you? What are you doing here?" asked Detective Howard.

"Hello, Detective Howard. I'm doing better. I'm sorry to intrude, but I wanted to check on the Williams girl, maybe talk to her."

"When the receptionist called to say Miss Williams had a visitor, we were a little alarmed. I know the girl has no real family and the only visitors have been few and far between. We have had officers posted here since the assault in the event that whoever did this to that poor girl returns to finish the job." said Howard.

"I completely understand, Detective Howard. Sloanne tells me that Miss Williams is waking up. Can she speak yet?"

"It's the damndest thing. Her doctor says she can communicate in writing, but she won't. I think maybe she is afraid and I don't blame her, but the information she has in her head may be the very thing we need to crack this case wide open," replied Howard.

"Do you think I could give it a try?" Chloe inquired of Howard.

"We haven't gotten anything out of her so I don't see how it could hurt," he replied, "Let's take a ride up."

The small group stepped onto the elevator and rode up in silence to the fourth floor. As Chloe stepped off the elevator, she saw one uniformed officer stationed at the nurse's desk and as they turned down the hallway toward Simone Williams' room, Chloe saw two more officers posted outside her door.

"We had her put in this room far enough away from the elevator and exit doors to thwart any potential attempt on Simone's life. Anyone who would try to get to her would have to get past us all," Detective Howard explained to Chloe.

"That seems very extreme, but then so does what was done to her," Chloe said.

"That was our thinking too. Anyone who would hurt

someone the way she was hurt, is liable to be desperate enough to try anything," Detective Howard said with disgust.

The group reached Simone's door and Detective Howard instructed Chloe to wait outside while he went in. He stepped inside the room and quietly closed the door behind himself. After only a few minutes he reappeared at the door and motioned Chloe to enter.

Chloe was afraid and uneasy, but determined as she made her way into the private room of Simone Williams. The unmistakable smell of disinfectant was strong in the room and the only sound heard was the beeping-hiss of the ventilator being used to help Simone breath.

In a chair in one corner of the room sat, who Chloe assumed, was a female, plainclothes officer who paid no attention to either of them as they entered the room. Detective Howard walked over to the officer and tapped her on the shoulder and she simply stood up and exited the room.

Chloe turned to the bed at her left and took in, for the first time, the pitiful sight of Simone Williams. The girl was so small the machines and tubes, which no doubt helped save her life, literally swallowed her tiny figure whole. Chloe stepped up to the bed and could see the full scale of the damage inflicted on the girl.

One side of Simone's head was shaved and all that remained was a massive surgical scar where a procedure to release fluid and pressure on her brain had been performed. The hair that was left behind was matted with blood and Betadine. One eye socket was crushed and another surgical scar with stitches was visible there. Her jaw appeared to be wired in such a way as to allow the ventilator room to fit down the girl's throat. There was a flattening of the girl's features on one side, that distorted Simone's face to an almost unrecognizable state and yet Chloe could see the girl was still beautiful.

Chloe tried to hold back the tears as she looked into Simone's eyes, but found the attempt, useless. She reached down and gently took the small hand of the girl and then began to speak.

"Hello, Simone. My name is Chloe Jacobs. I know you don't know me, but I had a little girl named Danni who was murdered." Chloe sobbed uncontrollably as Detective Howard watched Simone's eyes fill with tears. Chloe continued.

"Whoever killed my baby did horrible things to her. They hurt her and now that person has taken three other little girls and no one knows where they are. The police think whoever did this to you, may have killed my Danni."

Chloe broke down and fell to her knees on the floor beside the child's bed. As she held Simone's hand and cried, she continued speaking.

"I could not save my baby girl, but I think *you* can save those other, three girls. Please, Simone, tell us who did this to you."

As Chloe cried, Detective Howard turned away. He could not

handle the emotional scene and the pain this mother must be feeling. Somehow he felt responsible and it hurt him they could not save Danielle Jacobs.

Chloe felt Simone's hand shift and the small girl placed it softly on Chloe's head. As Chloe raised her eyes to Simone's, she saw the tears that streamed down the broken face of the girl. Simone then motioned for a pen and paper. Chloe jumped up and startled Detective Howard.

"A pen and paper, she wants to write something," Chloe demanded.

Detective Howard fumbled inside his coat and produced a small pad and a pen, handing them to Chloe who then helped Simone hold them.

As Simone wrote slowly, Chloe turned to Detective Howard with eyes wide as she read aloud the words on the paper.

I know him. Can identify picture. Seen him at work…big tipper.

Chloe whispered to Detective Howard to get a picture of Skip Perryman.

Detective Howard looked at her as if she was insane, but before he could speak, Chloe asked, "Do you trust Sloanne?"

"Of course I do," he replied.

"Then I need that photo," Chloe demanded.

Detective Howard immediately turned and quickly walked

from the room. As he did, Chloe turned back to Simone.

"We're going to show you a picture, okay? If the man in the picture is the man who did this to you, will you tell us?" Chloe asked the girl.

Simone squeezed Chloe's hand and weakly nodded, *yes*. As the two waited for Detective Howard to return, Chloe asked Simone if it would be okay for her to stay awhile and Simone again squeezed Chloe's hand and nodded.

Several minutes passed and finally Detective Howard returned with four, black and white photos printed out on standard, copy paper. Chloe took a deep breath, turned to Simone and began holding up each photo in turn.

She asked Simone, "Do you recognize any of these men?"

Simone's face instantly took on a look of terror as she viewed the photo that Chloe held up of Skip. Simone fumbled for the pen and paper lying on the bed. Chloe handed both to the girl and then Simone wrote the words, *That is him…the man who hurt me.*

Chloe bent close to Simone's face and asked, *"Are you certain?"*

Simone Williams wrote one word in response, *Yes*!

Chloe turned to Detective Howard and said, "It's him. Skip Perryman is your man."

Before she could finish the sentence, Detective Howard was running, full speed, out the door to catch a killer.

CRUELTY TO INNOCENTS

TWENTY-THREE

Cellar

The beautiful, small voices that called out to Shawn were the most welcoming sound he ever heard. Shawn looked back at Sloanne with fear and joy on his face. At first he seemed to hesitate, but a split second later, he was flying down the dark steps into the unknown of the cellar. Sloanne tried to slow him down, but she never got the opportunity to say anything before he was out of sight.

Sloanne was two steps behind Shawn. The dampness of the dark void made the air feel heavy, as the two felt their way through the pitch black in search of a light switch. Three, tiny voices that began whimpering quietly were now screaming and crying, making it difficult for Shawn and Sloanne to hear much else. Finally, Sloanne located a bare bulb that hung from the center of the space and pulled the chain dangling from it. As their eyes adjusted to the light, Sloanne took in the full horror of the cellar and the secrets it held.

Along one wall, the two Tyler twins were tied and blindfolded and on another wall, sat a young girl who Sloanne assumed was the latest victim from Havre de Grace. She was bound in the same manner as the other girls. In the center of the room was the unmistakable sexual torture device that was identified in the medical examiners report. Off to the left, a video camera was set up

274

with a large spotlight to allow someone to film their sexual exploits with the unwilling victims.

Just as Sloanne realized the full extent of the scene before her, Skip Perryman stepped out from a secluded alcove. In his right hand was a large, automatic pistol and in the other was a bottle of expensive scotch. Sloanne and Shawn immediately froze in their tracks as Skip grinned at them both.

"Hello, darlin', miss me?" Skip leeringly said to Sloanne. He then turned and said directly to Shawn, "Hello, lover boy. Didn't your mother ever tell you not to bring a knife to a gun fight?"

Skip's eyes then dropped to the large ax in Shawn's hands at the same time Shawn's eyes locked on the large pistol.

Sloanne was horrified as she looked into the face of the psychopath.

"How could you do this? What kind of monster are you? You know you will never get away with this," she nearly screamed at Skip.

"Oh, but I already have gotten away with this, darlin'," Skip said as he motioned for Shawn to drop the ax.

Shawn looked at Sloanne with an expression that said 'I'm so sorry' as he laid the ax down on the dirt floor.

"You can still get away, Skip. Nobody else needs to get hurt. If you're as smart as you think you are, you'll leave now before the police show up," Shawn said quietly as he shifted himself to a position that blocked Skip's view of Sloanne.

Sloanne realized Shawn was trying to place himself between her and the gun Skip held in his hand.

"You think you're so cool, don't you, lover boy? Get your mother fucking ass over on that wall right there," Skip growled at Shawn.

Shawn slowly moved toward the wall leaving Sloanne right in Skip's line of fire.

"I'm not going to leave here without these girls, Skip," Shawn said as he moved.

"Yeah, and if you say another word, I promise you will all leave here together...in body bags. Now get your ass over against that wall."

The three, young girls were hysterical by this point. They were crying and screaming. Fear was almost a living entity permeating the air in the cellar and filling Sloanne with a dread she had never known before.

"Skip, Please! What are you doing? These children have done nothing to you. Let them go, please," Sloanne pleaded with Skip.

"I'm sorry, Sloanne, but I'm afraid we just can't do that. Sometimes it doesn't matter that you haven't done anything wrong," Skip cooed at Sloanne.

"But why, Skip? Why are you doing this?"

"You could ask any question in the world and the best you can come up with is, why?" Skip replied as he moved quickly to Sloanne's side.

He moved like a cat as he slipped behind her and placed his arm around her waist, jerking her back against his body. His touch made Sloanne almost physically ill. Here was the monster who killed her Danni, standing beside her as if he were totally innocent.

Shawn did not miss the sickening way Skip grabbed Sloanne and he jerked as if to approach them, but then drew back eyeing again the pistol in Skip's hand.

"No, no, no, lover boy! You stay right where you are unless you two want to join Danni," Skip said with a grin.

Sloanne felt herself getting light-headed and had to consciously stop the spinning in her head.

Skip placed his lips close to Sloanne's ear and said, "You really want to know why? It's really very simple, darlin'. Because I can do whatever I like. I wanted your sweet little Danni and I took her."

"You didn't have to kill her," Sloanne almost sobbed out.

"No! Maybe if you would have come back here with me that night at the restaurant, like I asked you to do, I would have been a little nicer to that girl. But you thought you were too good for ol' Skip. She didn't have to die, you know. It should have been you, Sloanne. Let's see how well you sleep at night knowing Danni's death was your fault. I could easily have killed you in her place, but you didn't want to be with me anymore. So I did the next best thing, I killed your sweet little Danni. I knew her death would hurt you like you hurt me. I just wanted to be with you one more time. You should have listened to me, Sloanne."

Sloanne could hear Skip's voice as he talked and she could tell he was about to lose whatever bit of sanity he still had. She was even more afraid now.

"You didn't have to kill Danni. You could have just let her go. What was the point of murdering her, Skip?"

"She was going to ruin everything. She just kept talking and talking and talking. She was never going to shut up. All she was worried about where those two," Skip said as he pointed to the bound figures of Kimmi and Kammi.

"She broke the rules, Sloanne. We told them and told them to stop talking, but that little bitch would not shut up. I had to do something to shut her up and I did."

"Who is we?" Sloanne asked.

Skip's laugh nearly turned Sloanne's blood cold and the look on his face now was one of sheer lunacy. She couldn't figure out who Skip was talking about. She thought maybe he was schizophrenic or had a multiple personality disorder. It was the only explanation she could come to.

"Skip, this doesn't have to go any further. We can get you

some help,"

"Help! I don't need any help. I'm taking care of these little girls without any help at all. Look how happy they are to see me. You still don't understand do you, Sloanne? These girls love ol' Skip, they want him. Just like you used to. And I know how to treat them. Real nice and gentle. You remember how it was, Sloanne. You used to love it when I touched you. You were a wild thing back in those days. Too bad you've polluted yourself with that scum bag over there."

Skip ranted as he motioned towards Shawn. Sloanne could see nothing left of the man she once loved. He was completely gone and in his place was this monster.

"You piece of shit. You are a sick fucker and I will kill you myself if you hurt anyone else," Shawn yelled out.

Sloanne knew Shawn was trying to distract Skip and she stood transfixed and listened. She felt like she was in a nightmare with no way out.

"Shut your fucking mouth before I shoot a hole in you. You're the reason Sloanne doesn't want to be with me anymore. I have something special in mind for you, lover boy. Maybe a swim in the bay will close that mouth," Skip said as he approached Shawn.

He raised the gun up and brought it down with a vengeance, smacking Shawn hard on the left temple. Shawn fell to the ground, dazed from the blow, blood oozing from the wound.

"Skip, please. Don't hurt him, please." Sloanne cried out.

"I should kill him now just because you don't want me to," Skip replied.

"The police are on their way, Skip. They know. Simone Williams is waking up" Sloanne said.

"That girl won't be talking to anyone for a long time. I made sure of it."

"No. She is waking up, Skip. She's probably talking to the police right now."

"Damn it. I should have killed her when I had the chance,"

As the voices from the crying girls began to chew into Skip's brain, Sloanne could see how far from sanity he slipped, as he turned and yelled, "*Shut up,* all of you, so I can think."

Skip began to sway back and forth, rubbing the barrel of the gun up and down his temple as if trying to concentrate on the conversation. He was so far gone that Sloanne expected him to shoot them all at any minute and she silently prayed Patty and the police would show up to end this nightmare.

Skip seemed to be in a world of his own as he turned to Sloanne and pointed the gun at her. Shawn saw his opportunity and jumped towards Skip, grabbing at the gun and the two began to scuffle.

Sloanne ran toward the single girl and began to untie her. She could hear punches and the shuffling of the dirt as Skip and Shawn fought for possession of the gun. Sloanne grabbed the girl and dragged her over to where the twins were tied. She shoved the girl between the two tied girls and bent over them, shielding them all with her body. Just then, a single shot rang out and all three girls screamed. Sloanne was deafened by the sound of the gun and the smell of gunpowder filled her nose. She looked back to the two fighting men in time to see Shawn's body crumple to the dirt. Sloanne screamed and tried to get to Shawn, but Skip stepped over Shawn's prone body and pointed the gun directly at his head.

Just as the features of Skip's face twisted into a leering grin, Sloanne heard, "FREEZE!"

There stood Patty, gun drawn and leveled directly at Skip's chest.

TWENTY-FOUR

Betrayed

Sloanne never felt more relief than in those few seconds. She smiled at Patty, but he didn't acknowledge her, still keeping his eyes trained on Skip. Skip still held the gun in his hand, pointing at Shawn's head.

"Ah, the Cavalry is here to save us all. How's it going, Uncle Patty?" Skip leered at Patty.

"Drop the gun, Skip" Patty demanded.

"Yes, sir. Whatever you say, sir. But can I just hurt this asshole a little bit more?"

With that, Skip bent down and placed his thumb over the gushing hole in Shawn's leg and proceeded to prod the wound roughly. Shawn groaned in pain as Skip's finger disappeared into the hole.

Sloanne looked at Patty as if to ask why he was allowing this to go on, just as Patty yelled, "Enough, we don't have time for this. Sloanne, are you okay?"

Sloanne's face betrayed her confusion as Skip's wide grin seemed out of place for a man who had been caught committing a heinous murder.

"Well, Patty, are you going to tell your pretty niece all about our little association, or should I?" Skip asked leeringly.

Sloanne's mind was racing in a thousand different directions. What did Skip mean by 'association'? Sloanne could not even fathom what was happening and she was afraid to move, afraid to speak.

"Shut up, you piece of shit. This is all your fault. You couldn't control yourself. I should have killed you weeks ago," Patty hissed at Skip.

Skip began to laugh. It was a crazy, insane laugh that crept up Sloanne's spine and goosed the flesh on her arms.

Shawn looked at Sloanne through a haze of pain and saw the confusion on her face, the denial of the facts that were now becoming quite clear to him. The monster they had been searching for all this time was right under their noses. The grief and fear he felt for Sloanne was almost overwhelming.

"Patty?" Sloanne breathed, looking at her always-loving godfather.

The range of emotions Shawn saw on her face was heart-wrenching and he had to look away.

"Oh, kiddo! You always were just like your dad. He was always too inquisitive too," Patty said to Sloanne.

"I tried to keep you out of this, but you couldn't leave it alone. You should have stayed in New York, in your pretty, safe life. You never should have come back to this town." Patty said now.

Sloanne couldn't believe what she was hearing.

"Patty, what have you done? How could you be a part of this awful thing?" Sloanne asked in anguish. She was still standing next to the girls and she asked, "How could you, of all people, hurt these children this way?"

Patty looked at Sloanne with a life full of pain and hurt evident on his face and began to speak.

"This fucking genius used my company to order all of his disgusting equipment. I watched him for months, unsure of what he was planning. And then one day, he finally crossed the line. He took a girl, but not just any girl. He took Danni. I knew I had to step in and I followed him back here and the rest is, shall we say, history. I couldn't very well leave him to do this alone. I had to protect these girls, the way I've always protected you. The way a father should protect his daughter."

Sloanne's mind was reeling now. Patty said 'Father' and the thought sent anger boiling up inside Sloanne as she yelled, "Erin Kelly was my father. You don't have what it takes to be a father. No father would do this to his child. You are *sick*."

"Yes. Your mother said the same thing to me once. She said she had fallen in love with someone else. That what we had meant nothing to her. *Nothing*! She married Erin Kelly and you came along a few months later. He never even questioned it. He never even asked who your real father was. He just pretended you were his. Your mother made me promise never to tell and in return, I could remain a part of your life."

"No. You're lying. My mother would never do that. She was a good person." Sloanne cried.   Sloanne could not believe that her wonderful, loving godfather was actually her father and the man who raised and loved her...wasn't.

"She would, and did! Do you have any idea what it is like watching another man live your life day in and day out? Watching him raise your child as his own. Watching as the only woman you ever loved, loves another man. And worst of all, watching her die because of your mistakes."

"This is priceless! I never would have known what a twisted, sick fuck you really are, Patrick. I'm glad I got to be in on this. What fun!" Skip laughingly said.

"Shut up, you bastard. If it weren't for your sick obsessions, we wouldn't be here now," Patty threw back at Skip.

Sloanne was so overwhelmed with grief and anguish she couldn't even cry. She looked at Shawn fearing he may bleed to death, but her mind started to work on the revelations Patty was divulging. She could not believe the father she'd known and loved all her life wasn't really her father. If what Patty was saying was true, she lived her whole life in the midst of a lie. One big lie.

"Seems your daddy here has been 'protecting' little girls for a long time now. All the way back to New York, isn't that right, daddy?"

285

Skip looked at Patty with disdain and grinned.

"You took those kids in New York? It was you? What did you do with them, Patty?"

Sloanne could not believe the man who loved and protected her all her life was a kidnapper of children.

"I loved every one of those girls like their parents should have. Every one of them is living a better life today because of me. Because I loved them. None of them was ever you, Sloanne. None of them could ever take your place. When your 'dad' started snooping around in New York, spending all his spare time searching for the person who took them, I couldn't let him find out. I had to stop him."

"What do you mean, you had to 'stop' him?" Sloanne asked Patty now.

"Your dad never knew it was me, Sloanne. I knew he was getting close and I had to stop him. But he was your mother's husband and your father. I didn't want you two to be hurt. I knew I couldn't kill him, but I had to slow him down."

The reality began to sink into Sloanne's mind. She said more to herself than to Patty, "You shot my father? You did it to keep him from figuring out what a monster you are. You were his friend and his partner. He loved you. He would have died for you."

Patty dropped his eyes as if the shame were too much for him. He began to speak.

"I thought it would all be over after that. I thought Erin

would let it go and start a new life here in Aberdeen. I hoped we could all just go on with our lives. But he never did let it go. It was by sheer coincidence that I got the call that day, from that detective in New York. He wanted to change the appointment time your father set up with him. I had to find a way to end his snooping for good. I thought maybe if I could get rid of him, your mother and I would have a chance to find our way back to one another. That we could finally be a family. But things didn't work out the way I planned. Your mom was never supposed to be in that car. I never meant to hurt her. I loved her more than my own life."

Sloanne's eyes now welled with tears as she slid down the wall beside the three little girls. The girls closed their arms around her as she sobbed uncontrollably. Shawn crawled through the dirt to reach Sloanne and the girls as Patty looked on. Shawn could see the finality on Patty's face. He knew Patty was a monster, but he had no doubt Patty still loved Sloanne. Patty turned his eyes from Shawn and then trained his gun on Skip.

"What are you doing, old man?" Skip asked with shock in his voice.

Without a second's hesitation, Patty simply said, "Ending it once and for all," and he pulled the trigger.

Shawn held tight to Sloanne and the girls as he braced for the gun shot.

As Patty pulled the trigger, everything seemed to move in

slow motion. The bullet hit Skip Perryman dead-on in the forehead and exited through the back of his skull, rocking his head back into the stone wall. As the bullet passed through Skip's brain tissue, it splintered his skull spewing brain and skull fragments over the wall in the exact place Danielle Jacobs had taken her last breath.

The three girls were no longer screaming, seemingly in shock, but clung together in Sloanne's arms. Shawn still held them all together. The echo of the gun blast tapered off and Sloanne could hear the faint sound of ringing that quickly turned to the sound of sirens wailing in the distance.

Patty walked over to the group on the floor and Sloanne looked up into the face of the man she loved. The man who helped raise her. She had never really known this man and her heart broke as she saw tears fall from Patty's eyes.

"I have always loved you, Sloanne. No matter what you discover, no matter what anyone ever tells you, it has always been about you. I will always love you," Patty said solemnly.

Without another word, Patty turned and shot the light bulb that hung in the center of the room. Darkness poured through the space like water.

Shawn and Sloanne heard the faint shuffling of Patty's feet on the dirt floor. And then there was silence.

Within a few moments, a rush of footsteps could be heard above them and a light shone down into the darkness from the top of the stairs.

"Sloanne, Shawn, can you hear me?"

Detective Howard's voice was clear and strong and beautiful.

TWENTY-FIVE

Saved

The light from the top of the stairs grew closer and what sounded like a thousand footsteps could be heard moving swiftly above Sloanne and Shawn, with the word, 'clear', being shouted from one officer to another. A flashlight panned the room then stopped on the huddled group.

"We need help down here. Shawn has been shot," yelled Sloanne to the light.

The light from above was blinding and Sloanne put her hand up to shield from the brightness.

"Check everywhere. He's gotten away," Sloanne yelled again as the sounds of running echoed down the stairs.

"Sloanne, Skip Perryman is dead. He won't be going anywhere ever again," Detective Howard yelled back.

"Not Perryman, Patrick Louchlin!" Sloanne screamed.

Detective Howard jerked back as if he had been slapped. How could Sloanne think that Patty had anything to do with this horrible crime? He fixed his lips to speak just as Sloanne cut him off.

"It is Patty, Detective Howard. Find him. He's your kidnapper," replied Sloanne.

With that Detective Howard turned and ran back to the stairs, yelling instruction to his men above.

"We need a search of the grounds immediately. Locate Patrick Louchlin." Detective Howard instructed. He turned to Sloanne and asked, "Is he armed?"

"Yes," was Sloanne's only word.

Detective Howard continued barking orders, "The subject is to be considered armed and dangerous. We need some light down here and a medic, ASAP. Jenkins, get on the horn and call for an APB on Louchlin. Have the other crew check out his home and also his business. This guy is liable to be anywhere now that he knows we're on to him. Wake up Judge Carson. We need a court order to seize Louchlin's bank account. Maybe we can cut him off before he gets too far."

Immediately, light and movement flooded the small space and the room above, as police brought in flood lights and placed them about the room. Detective Howard moved to Shawn's side followed closely by an EMT.

"He's lost a good deal of blood, but I think he'll be okay," Sloanne said as she looked into Shawn's face and smiled.

The medical technicians immediately began to work on Shawn's leg and the injury to his head.

"Are any of you injured?" the EMT asked Sloanne trying to assess the need for more medical attention for the huddled group.

"No, we aren't wounded. Girls?"

Sloanne tried to raise the head of one of the three, shivering children, but they all clung even tighter to her.

"They have been through a great deal, but they aren't hurt. They're scared, but not hurt," she said.

"Can you stand up?" Detective Howard asked Sloanne in a soft voice.

"Yes. Girls, I need for you all to listen to me now. These people are here to help and no one can hurt you ever again. We're saved." Sloanne quietly said to the little girls.

The three little faces looked up slowly into Sloanne's and all three had a look of uncertainty as Shawn began to speak from behind them.

"Kimmi, Kammi, this is Sloanne. This is Uncle Shawn's very good friend and you can trust her."

With that, the three girls began to cry and relaxed their tight grip on Sloanne enough to stand and walk out with her.

"This guy is a mess. We'll need a shovel to get this guy's head in a bag," came the voice of an ME behind Sloanne.

Another ME spoke in turn, "Too bad we couldn't have found the other guy. Can you believe it? The guy used to be a cop. How could he have done something like this?"

"I don't know, but he deserves to be in a bag as much as this guy," came the reply.

Sloanne listened to the two men and a great sorrow filled her. How could the man she had known and loved all her life, have done this terrible thing? She was devastated at the knowledge she had never really known Patrick Louchlin.

"Let's get this guy off the wall," said the first ME and the two proceeded to process the body of Skip Perryman.

"Okay, let's get the stairway cleared. We need to get this guy upstairs and to the hospital," an EMT shouted as both ends of the gurney supporting Shawn were raised and moved towards the bottom of the staircase.

As the gurney passed by Sloanne and the three girls, Shawn smiled his crooked smile and said, "There's my girls."

His two nieces hugged him so tight he could hardly breathe, but it was the very best hug he ever had. As the gurney carrying Shawn began to be lifted up the stairs, Sloanne bent and placed a kiss on his lips.

"Thank you, Sloanne. We never would have found them if you had not been here." Shawn whispered to her.

"You just worry about getting fixed, Mr. Macho. I will be right behind you, okay."

Sloanne breathed back to Shawn with a smile.

"You better be," he replied as the gurney proceeded up the stairs.

As Sloanne and the girls started up the stairs, the three girls all turned to her as if unsure. Sloanne looked up to the top of the stairway and then back to the girls.

"Are you ready?" she gently asked.

Each little girl nodded her head and the four made their way up to the open cellar door. As Sloanne and the girls moved across the small living room, remnants of Skip's presence were evident everywhere. Sloanne saw flashes of light coming through the open door from outside. She realized they were camera flashes and she turned to Detective Howard with a concerned look on her face.

"The media is here already?" she asked Detective Howard.

"Birney Sullivan, that guy never misses a story," was Detective Howard's reply. "He called the girls' parents too. The twins' parents are already here and Hailey's family should be here any minute."

Sloanne smiled to herself. She had been so wrong about Birney Sullivan. She had been wrong about many things. She was deep in thought as a tiny hand reached up and pulled her sleeve. Sloanne quickly knelt to Kimmi Tyler as the child began to speak.

"Did you see her? Did she send you?"

"Did who send me, baby?" Sloanne asked uneasily.

"The angel. Danni, the angel! She said she would save us. She said she would never leave us."   Kimmi's pure, innocent voice poured into Sloanne's ear as she remembered the dream of Danni's voice whispering to her, '*You're almost there...*'

Tears flooded Sloanne's eyes and spilled over her cheek as she said the words, "Yes, baby, I saw her. Danni sent me to you."

The little girl smiled and whispered, "I knew it."

Sloanne stood to walk out the door and voices began to shout the girls' names. Every officer present on the scene, stopped to watch the beautiful sight as three girls ran, full-speed, into the waiting arms of the families they almost lost.

EPILOGUE

In the days and months that followed the 9-1-1 abductions, many things changed in Aberdeen Maryland and in Sloanne Mae Kelly's life. The three children who were saved from Patrick Louchlin and Skip Perryman were back in school and all three were in therapy for the abuse they suffered at the hands of the two pedophiles.

Rochelle Perryman was implicated in the crimes as an accessory after the fact, for allowing Skip to use the vacant property for his illegal activities. John Perryman did what he probably should have done years ago; he filed for divorce and left Rochelle high and dry. The local newspaper had gotten hold of the story and photos of Rochelle Perryman being carted away in handcuffs splashed the front page of the *Aberdeen Chronicle*. Birney Sullivan was later presented with a prestigious award for excellence in journalism. He was offered a position as a correspondent for a national network for his write up and participation in the 9-1-1 abductions rescue and story. Birney Sullivan could now be seen every night on the evening news as a field reporter for a major national network.

Chloe had gone back to work and was trying to live her life, one day at a time without her beautiful Danni. She had gotten a little help from Detective Howard who was now the person she spent her evenings with and the two fit together nicely as a couple.

Simone Williams had become very close with Chloe in the days and weeks following the 9-1-1 abductions and upon her release from the hospital, she had given up her apartment and moved in with Chloe as a roommate and was back in school full time. She made it a point to find the two boys who saved her in the park and the groups were now fast friends.

As for Sloanne, she had gone back to New York, but not to stay. She had chosen someone whom Mr. Miera trusted to run Miera Architecture and sold her shares of the business to the active members of the board. Sloanne sold her apartment, gathered all her belongings and headed back to live in her hometown of Aberdeen. Shawn had given up his apartment as well and moved into Sloanne's parents' home, the home they would share together. The injuries that Shawn received as a result of the gunshot wound had been enough to end any chance of him continuing on as a fireman and he had been given an early pension and retirement due to his injuries.

The Aberdeen police department awarded Sloanne Mae Kelly and Shawn William Tyler, the civilian equivalent of The Medal of Valor, for their role in finding and rescuing the abducted children. Harford county had gone one step further and offered Sloanne a job as a consultant doing investigative work for not only the Aberdeen police department, but for other area agencies as well. With the help of her new assistant, Shawn Tyler, the two soon opened *Saving Angels Investigative Agency.*

CRUELTY TO INNOCENTS

A memorial had been erected in the Aberdeen City Park as a tribute to Danielle Jacobs and the courage she had shown in sacrificing her own life for the twin girls Kimmi and Kammi Tyler. The ceremony had been beautiful and attended by over twenty thousand people. Simone Williams, Kimmi and Kammi Tyler and Hailey Carver, the four girls who survived the fateful 9-1-1 abductions were there to unveil the statue, a beautiful girl with wings, her arms outstretched to the heavens. The inscription below it read: An Angel Touched Us and We Will Never Forget Danielle Jacobs 1996-2009

Patty has never been caught and not a single trace of his whereabouts has ever been found. The search of his home later revealed all of the children he took from New York so many years prior, were sold to families or individuals around the globe. He had been saving his profits from the sale of those children for years. This money was withdrawn on the very day that Sloanne and Shawn found the missing girls and it was widely presumed the money was Patty's lifeline. Patty's business and belongings were confiscated and auctioned off by the county with some of the proceeds going to the Aberdeen police and surrounding agencies to train each and every member of the force in child abduction cases. All remaining proceeds were donated to The *National Center for Missing and Exploited Children* on behalf of Danielle Jacobs and the children who have never been found.

CRUELTY TO INNOCENTS

The search for the missing children and their whereabouts are *Saving Angel's* main focus now. Sloanne and Shawn vowed to not only find and help prosecute Patty for his treacherous deeds, but locate every child and reunite them with the families from which they were taken.

****

The woman sat at the red light and watched in horror as a man was shot just a few feet away from her passenger-side window. The kid who shot the man paid her no attention as he made quick work of emptying the bleeding man's pockets. He then turned and made his way down the alley, disappearing over a fence and was gone.

She turned to her daughter who was deep in thought, focusing on her coloring book and said calmly, "Don't move, okay?"

The young mother jumped from her vehicle and ran quickly to the side of the critically injured man who lay helpless on the city sidewalk. She had taken CPR and first aid, but feared her knowledge would never be enough to help this poor man. She tried anyway.

A crowd began to gather on the street and sidewalk and the headlights of a half dozen cars flooded the space where she tried feverishly to save the dying man. The crowd grew thick and completely enveloped the woman and the man whose life she was attempting to save. Just behind the crowd, unnoticed by any of the onlookers, a flash of light broke the darkness then disappeared. One more flash of light came, the flicker of a lighter. The small girl looked up and into the eyes of a stranger. He smiled at her and she smiled back...and she was gone!

ABOUT THE AUTHORS

CK Webb was born and raised in Mississippi, and dreamed of writing like the greats; Emily Bronte, Edgar Allen Poe, and Stephen King, to name a few. CK joined the US Navy and traveled the world, but eventually returned to settle down in the tiny town of Millport, Alabama. A self-proclaimed 'reformed bad girl', this thirty-something writer now shares her life with her husband and two beautiful children. CK also enjoys spending time with her friends, family, and book club. Although CK delights in preying on the fears of others and enjoys killing people…thankfully she does it the legal way; in her novels. She has just completed the first two novels in the *Innocents* series which she co-wrote with her best-friend and mother, DJ Weaver. CK writes in a variety of other genres and also writes articles and book reviews for *Suspense Magazine*.

DJ Weaver is a fledgling author who has recently realized a long time goal, and completed her first two novels in the *Innocents* series, which she co-wrote with her daughter and best friend, CK Webb. The novels are the first two in a planned series of three books. DJ also writes in a variety of other genres. When she isn't writing, DJ develops and maintains WebbWeaver Review blog and Interview site. She also serves as co-chairwoman of WebbWeaver Book Club. DJ is a voracious reader, and also enjoys spending time with her friends, family and grandchildren. DJ also writes book reviews for

Suspense Magazine.

http://theinnocents.weebly.com

http://webbweaver-zelda555.blogspot.com/

www.ingramcontent.com/pod-product-compliance
Lightning Source LLC
Chambersburg PA
CBHW020915200626
46814CB00001BA/342